the adventures of a Jane Austen addict

Sex & Sensibility

the adventures of a Jane Austen addict

—a novel by—

ROSEMARIE SANTINI

SAINT BOOKS
New York

Direct any inquiries to
SAINT BOOKS
P.O. Box 865
Village Station
New York, NY 10014
saintbooks@earthlink.net

ISBN 0-9764111-0-5

Library of Congress Control Number: 2005900844

Printed in the United States of America.

Jacket & interior design and composition by
MULBERRY TREE PRESS, INC.
(www.mulberrytreepress.com)

1 3 5 7 9 10 8 6 4 2

for Florence Belsky

Prologue

I USED TO LOVE SKATING alongside the Hudson River. Though the highway was crowded, and the bumpy concrete made for precarious maneuvering, I'd sneak out of our West Village apartment when I was supposed to be doing homework. Dressed to the nines even then in jeans, T-shirt, and fringed vest, I'd lace up my expensive new skates for my run—depositing my ballet shoes in our mailbox for safekeeping.

I'd soar down Perry Street, knowing that I only had an hour before winter darkness set in—and with it, the strange waterfront goings-on Mom warned me about. And I'd hold up my arms in a Christ-like motion, expecting the congested traffic to stop for me so I could cross the highway.

Almost always, it did.

I'd have my run—up one block, then turn and back again. Sometimes drivers would smile, sometimes frown. A few clapped while several gave me the finger, but I didn't care. I was on my own, marking my own route, curly hair flying, my body safe and sure.

Flying high!

One rainy afternoon, I ran smack into a homeless man who'd taken an unexpected turn with his cart. I doubled over and hit the ground, lucky that it was dirt and not concrete. But I clipped my nose on the cart, and blood came streaming forth.

In that instant I transformed from flying girl to whimpering baby. There was only one place I wanted to be, and that was home.

My mother was chopping celery in the kitchen. "What happened?" she shouted, making defensive motions with the large knife in her hand.

"I f-fell," I said, stumbling over the very words.

Mom did all the right things—cleaning away the blood on my face, feeling around for broken bones, deciding there were none—but we ran over to St. Vincent's Emergency just in case.

A young intern said I needed stitches.

I began to weep.

Mom said, "Lizzie, stop being such a coward." She went on to cite every feminist icon from the goddess Isis to Gloria Steinem as the brave *New Women* of the future.

"You are one of them. My daughter will change the world," she boasted to the confused intern.

"She's really hurting," he admonished.

So Mom leaned closer to me and said, "Lizzie, please don't cry. It'll ruin my makeup."

Somehow, I sucked it up . . .

That night, when Dad came home from his important producer's job at Sam Shapiro's film company, I was in bed reading Jane Austen. Mom's accusations were muted, but I knew she was asking him why he was so late. He grumbled his usual excuses, then heard today's news flash and rushed into my bedroom.

He put his arms around me in a great hug. "How's my princess?"

"Oh, Daddy, I'm ugly!" I cried, pointing to the large bandage around my nose before breaking into a loud wail.

"You'll never be ugly to me," he said softly. "Those tears falling on your cheeks—they're like diamonds. I'm going to catch them and put them right next to my heart, so they can sparkle every time it beats."

I felt better right away. "Mom says I shouldn't cry. She says I should be brave."

"Lizzie, if you feel like crying, just do it."

"But I don't want to be some stupid, silly girl," I mumbled and cried some more. "I want to be a heroine . . . like in Jane Austen's books."

He kissed my moist cheeks. "Then be like Jane."

I stared at him through my tears. "Huh?"

"Be funny—and everyone will love you!"

Sex in Manhattan

Chapter One

— 1 —

GOSH! This is hard to do.

Harry Archer's lips were sort of exploring a part of my anatomy not usually offered for public consumption—or should I say *pubic* consumption?

Oops!

Hey, that isn't nice!

I absolutely swore that I would not lose my head while getting it on with Harry Archer, who happens to be my editor-in-chief while also happening to be the cutest guy on my horizon since Billy De Luca of the beautiful dark eyes and muscular body stole my heart at my high school prom.

Yes, that was a long time ago, but though I'd "experienced men" since sweet sixteen, I'd never come across anyone with the sexual charisma of Harry.

"Ohhhh!"

My lips began moving involuntarily as Harry did an excellent job of stirring things up. I thought—oh—yes!! Still, I was *veree* nervous. I hadn't been in love for ages and ages, and had only been flirting with the idea of flirting with Harry. It was dangerous because he was my boss. In these days of Political Correctness, our enjoyable encounter could be termed sexual harassment.

(This was an area I vowed never to get into. Besides, I was a freelancer. Could freelancers sue editors for sexual harassment? Hmmm. Maybe I should look that up.)

Well, this flirty eye thing with Harry had been going on since *The Record's* Oscar Night party, when several starlets attempted to poach him while he was ogling me. It was obvious to Fancy Murphy, my copyeditor, and Tony Palermo from public relations that something was about to burst.

"This is the night," Tony sang in my ear.

"Oh, no. I need to go home and polish a review." I turned pompous, sounding like my mother. "Work always comes first."

"Yeah, yeah, yeah," Fancy smart-mouthed.

— 2 —

WELL, I MEANT ALL I SAID. I had been trained to write film reviews by the great Edgar Meredith, who had worked for the revered *Los Angeles Times* then emigrated back to Gotham to teach at the New School University, where I had the good fortune to meet him whilst thinking of writing a novel which would involve a kind of modern-day Jane Austen sensibility.

"Harrumph," Edgar disparaged, "you mean *Bridget Jones*, *Clueless*—that kind of nonsense?"

"Yes," I said.

"I think a shift in career priorities is in order, young lady."

That's how I became a film reviewer, one of the most

competitive goals among Manhattan's writing community.
And I succeeded.

— 3 —

"A PENNY FOR YOUR THOUGHTS," Harry interrupted my
stream of consciousness. "Did you enjoy yourself, sweetie?"
Enjoy which part? What were we up to?
Oh shit! Sexual attention deficit.
My mind had wandered again. Whilst enjoying the physical entertainments of the body, my mind often decamped to
an intellectual level where thoughts and phrases encountered
in real life experience were recorded for use in my screenplay.
Today, however, I couldn't even process my words. I kept sulk-
ing about why I'd begun this thing with Archer, about how
and why I became a film reviewer . . . issues that had no place
in this time or this bed. Nor would stewing over these questions help write my scenario. Besides, it was crazy to be so
consumed with trivia a moment before. . . .
"Yes. Yes. Yes," I whispered.
Then Harry kissed me.
And I buried my face in his tangled locks.
Then . . . well, you know what happened.
It was lovely, fantastic, brilliant, classic. Through it all, my
mind was centered on one absolute, striking phrase which I
must report on at the next JANO (Jane-o-holics) meeting.

I turned to Harry, but before I could speak, he gestured to
a heart-shaped silver frame on my bedside table.
"Who's that handsome chap?"
"My dad."

"What's he do?"

"He used to work in films . . . don't know what he's up to these days."

"Oh? Out of touch?"

"You might say that."

My eyes began tearing. "God, I'm sorry!" Harry looked alarmed. "Didn't mean to . . ."

"Hey. I'm a big girl. I have a moisture problem in my eyes . . . nothing more." I bit on a quivering lip.

"I see."

I eyed Harry, who was lying back on my pillow. It was encased in a lovely Frette lace pillowcase which matched the trim from the sheets and the sweetpea design on the comforter. This bed setting was deliberately chosen to calm me down when my dreams raced out of control. Though not quite nightmares, these scenarios involved things like walking through Times Square in the middle of the night with no clothes on.

"My parents divorced when I was five. How old were you?" Harry asked.

Should I lie?

Harry filled the silence. "They sent me to a shrink."

"Did it help?"

"I hope so. And you?"

I shook my head. "You know who my mother is."

"The feminist author . . ."

I nodded. "Mom believes that our lives are political. Whenever I cried, she'd tell me to be brave."

Damn. My cheeks had somehow become covered with tears. *Stupid, silly girl.* Why are you being so personal?

Wisely, I kept my outburst inside my head, but it must have shown because Harry put his arms around me and whispered, "Are you all right, Lizzie?"

"Oh, yes," I obediently replied.

Then he held me close for a *veree* long moment.

— 4 —

I BEGAN TO THINK THAT HARRY might be different from all the men I knew when he quickly destroyed that fantasy with the eternal question of first-time lovers.

"Did you have a really good time?"

"Indeed," I replied sharply, happy that my emotions were under control again.

His voice got a little anxious. "Well, could you be a bit more excited about it?"

"You need more vivacious copy?" I joked, referring to our professional relationship, where he often made such demands.

"Lie a little. It'll be good for my ego."

I tried. "You're a *veree* sexy man, and it was amazing!"

"Better than . . . ?"

Oh, damn. Harry needed more reassurance. "I was just thinking . . ."

"About?" he prompted.

"You're a lovely man, Harry, and I know that you've read all of her work. So I wanted to tell you that I really think you're man enough for Jane Austen."

Harry burst out laughing.

"Lizzie, you are adorable," he said, starting to initiate our second round of sex, affection, whatever . . .

Damn it! He wasn't taking me seriously!

Instead, he was treating me like a sex object, whispering little phrases and touching me in all those special places, being sweet and tender and asking me ever so nicely what I liked, how I felt, what I wanted . . .

But I had just told him what I wanted, hadn't I?

I had just divulged my most secret wish, to have a lover who could take me in and out of Austenland, someone who had read the novels, who knew each and every phrasing that could—and would—turn me on.

Why wasn't he paying attention?

— 5 —

I CLASSIFY PEOPLE BY THEIR FAVORITE Jane Austen novel.

Fancy loved *Persuasion* and confessed to me that since she was a little girl, she'd dreamt about sailing the seas with a handsome man, whom she searched for everywhere but never met. Fancy spent a lot of time around Mystic, Connecticut with wealthy sports types who trolled the waters on expensive vessels. She was invited along on some of these sails, but when she returned, Fancy was not happy.

"Sure, they take a fancy to Fancy," she told me after one debacle. "But those yachtsmen are sea monsters. Every girl who goes on a sailing vessel is sport for the team."

"But Anne Elliott gets her guy in *Persuasion*," I consoled her. "Just keep hoping."

And she did . . . my kind of girl.

Tony Palermo favored *Mansfield Park* and was quite open about the fact that he was in love with his sister, Lena. He hoped she would never marry any of the men she dated.

"The book is about Mary and Henry Crawford, not at all about Fanny and Edmund," he'd insist, though I counted the amount of scenes the recent film adaptation gave to each duo and told him he was wrong.

Harry Archer, my brilliant editor-in-chief, had long ago admitted to adoring *Northanger Abbey*. "It's a novel about fiction itself," he said. Harry was secretly writing an epic. He planned to buy an island and never return to Gotham after he received an expected six million dollar sale.

When I asked him what his book was about, Harry smiled and said, "It's about you, Lizzie."

Oh, God.

As a boss Harry was pretty cool, allowing me all sorts of personal idiosyncrasies in my reviews. But as a beau, he was a jealous maniac, especially hard on any Austen hero I happened to be hot for. (Actually, I loved them all.)

Harry also challenged my favorite book, *Sense and Sensibility*, as a non-runner in the Austen sweepstakes. When I explained to him that the title denoted both sides of my elusive personality, he grumped and kept quiet for two or three sex sessions except to yell, "Yeah, baby," at his moment of climax.

– 6 –

LATER THAT DAY, FANCY CALLED. "Oh, God. I'm late. I need to get to the gym for two hours, go home, then change for my date with Dermot."

"Why don't you skip the gym?"

"Oh, I could never do that!"

I knew that Fancy was beyond appeal. Of late she'd fixated on the loose flesh of her upper arms because Dermot had delivered a point-by-point critique of her physical flaws after an evening of sex.

Yes, she'd agreed, they were a little flabby. That's when Dermot advised that a personal trainer might help Fancy achieve some leanness.

It was my personal opinion that most men were so self-

absorbed that they'd find any way to poison intimate relationships. Almost to a man, they'd unleash hyper-critical
minds to attack a lady's appearance after they'd had sex.

Our bodies!! Feminists had diligently worked to give Our
Bodies to Ourselves—and now every man in jockey shorts
worked fervently to take Our Bodies from Us. Not in the
normal way of *Lady Chatterley* fucking, but with this terrible
personal insecurity bit.

Not me. I had enough of the *Bridget Jones* flab psychosis.

Yes, I love Bridget, but she did go on and on about her
weight. Boring subject, I think.

But not to Fancy, who is preparing for liposuction despite
the fact that no insurance will pay for it.

And it was all for sex!

I vowed that would *never* happen to me.

For I had JANO to keep me on the path of Austen sensibility.

Chapter Two

— 1 —

IN A WORLD BESET BY TERRORISM, free fall econom-
ics, bad hairstyles, and huge divorce rates, a girl has to
have some kind of moral guide.

Sex and the City and *Bridget Jones* have contributed in
this department, but something is lacking in the "civility"
department.

For while it's true that the most direct path to bonding is
sex (not that there's anything wrong with this!!) there must be
something BEYOND SEX, mustn't there?

Something like sweetness and affection and respect?

Dismayed at the current mode of conduct, i.e. "Do what
you have to do, baby," which promises freedom and choice but
generally degenerates into simple permission to be UTTERLY
SELFISH (not that there's anything wrong with that sometimes), a few of us organized JANO as a checklist for our
behavior, a corrective, like the confessionals and torture
chambers of old—only hopefully more forgiving.

This group consists of Jane Austen addicts. Yes, this
clergyman's daughter who lived almost two centuries ago
still influences many of us. Consider all those films of her
novels!

In sophisticated societies, there are several reactions to Jane Austen:

1. The established JA fans (mostly academics) who discuss her literary importance and hold conferences around the world.
2. The artistic fans who produce books and films heavily influenced by her, i.e. *Bridget Jones* and *Clueless*.
3. The reverse types who wouldn't be seen dead reading her books because they are considered WOMEN'S BOOKS!!

JANO members fail all those categories. Our belief is that Jane Austen is part of human nature, that if you read her novels as a sort of bible your life will be replenished and soulful.

Living a JANO life takes balls . . . that's why we ask our members of both sexes:

ARE YOU BRAVE ENOUGH FOR JANE AUSTEN?

– 2 –

EVERY OTHER TUESDAY WE MET in Gabriel Graves' at the Gramercy Park Hotel, where his rooms overlooked the city's only gated, private park. Though the locale reflected late-nineteenth-century elegance and the Edith Wharton type of life, the hotel attracted rock stars, actors, fashion types, and rich kids like Gabriel who wanted to be all three.

His room was an eclectic mixture of expensive electronic toys—an Xbox, a Dreamcast, numerous game and music CDs, one desktop and two laptop computers, several audio components not even out of their boxes, and even more strange kinds of percussion instruments (Gabriel's music was *veree* percussive this month). Some sort of musical synthesizer lay half-disassembled in the corner, with a 1958 Les Paul Gibson guitar leaning over it.

Tonight I was early because I wanted a moment with Gabriel before the rest of the gang arrived. When I walked in, his door was half opened and the gorgeous chap was lying naked on a chaise longue reading *Emma* under a Rolling Stones poster where Mick Jagger was flaunting his buttocks.

On a Victorian table next to the chaise stood an Art Deco tray which held two blue champagne flutes, a tin of butter mints from England, and a split of Piper-Heidsieck 1990. This was for us.

In contrast, across the room a card table held a carafe of California Chablis, a half dozen bottles of beer on ice, three bottles of Pellegrino mineral water, and a two-liter bottle of supermarket cola. In a deep cardboard box I saw two large bags of potato chips, three of pretzels, and two jumbo plastic containers filled with Hershey's kisses. This was for the troops.

"Oh, great, Lizzie. You've come!" Gabriel said warmly. He was referring to the fact that he'd left several messages on my answering machine that he was ready for sex.

His body was perfect—Gabriel toned at a Bowery gym three times a day. He'd confessed when I met him that he was determined to have a body like Michelangelo's *David*. He'd succeeded, except that his sexual organ was almost always aroused, unlike the classic statue's limp position.

"Sweet girl, I have all the props you adore." He waved a copy of a magazine with my dream lad on the cover.

Oh, my.

I tried to play it cool.

"I've seen that, Gabriel."

"You probably sleep with it," he said sharply.

Unfortunately, he was right on the mark. I had a serious

crush on the Brit actor who specialized in deliciously naughty roles.

This was going to be seriously difficult.

Okay, Jane, what the hell do I do? I thought of Elizabeth Bennett finally telling off Fitzwilliam Darcy and wondered whether I could get away with that. Probably not.

"Ehhh." My throat felt dry. What a coward I was!

When I began speaking I squawked like a cracked chicken. "Gabriel, dear." He looked up suspiciously at that word which I rarely used. "I–I wanted to t-talk to you about us," I stuttered.

Somehow he knew what I'd been doing this morning. He sat up straightaway, throwing the magazine on the floor and stomping on it. "You've done it with someone else, you bitch!!"

"Angel?"

"Don't call me that," he sneered.

Oh-oh. His erection suddenly deflated. I worried about what he was feeling, because I knew from research that anger in males (along with appetite) caused erections. So what was he thinking now?

"We'll have to discuss this," Gabriel threatened.

"Must we?"

"Well, isn't that the point of JANO? You've betrayed Jane."

Too true.

Then he disappeared into the bathroom.

Oh, God! This was the stuff of our JANO meetings. Our main issue: How to act with civility in all sorts of situations, especially those that took place in the bedroom.

I walked over to the chaise and poured champagne into a blue crystal flute. I felt bad for sensitive men like Gabriel who adore Jane Austen, because it was hard for them to be macho in the usual ways. Gabriel's particular mentor/model was Mr. Knightley, who was kind, brotherly, and sincere to

Emma. Generally this was the way Gabriel behaved. In New York this meant people constantly labeled him as gay (not that there is anything wrong with that particular sexual preference).

I knew from firsthand experience that Gabriel had a rather agile dick which grew to ample proportions at the sight of female breasts, female buttocks, et al.

— 3 —

I'D MET GABRIEL IN The New School Library, where he was reading while uttering lascivious moans. When I saw the book was *Emma*, I immediately went over, introduced myself to him, spent three hours talking about Jane Austen, and landed in his bed that *veree* night.

Since I'd been celibate for a couple of years, this had been quite a feat . . . but then, reading Jane Austen is quite an aphrodisiac.

So I'd had two rounds of Gabriel's shagging (I do prefer this word to "fucking." Besides, fellow Americans who watch British films know what it means.)

When we broke off the first time, Gabriel joined JANO, complaining to everyone that I'd broken his heart, and it was never to mend. The actual truth was that after our breakup, Gabriel was soon involved sexually with all sorts of women— and perhaps men!

Whereas I had been celibate for ages and ages, only to leap on the plank with him again last week.

I know it's a poor excuse, but it was summer. It was hot. Gabe kept calling. Night after night, for a whole week, we had serious sex.

Then, on the weekend, Harry Archer entered my bed, and my heart.

Alas!

I betrayed my angel for a man I knew was going to hurt me (and possibly fire me into the bargain).

— 4 —

NOW AS I WAITED FOR GABRIEL to reappear I angsted over how he'd sussed out my infidelity. Was it my dour expression or my expanding breasts? Or had one of my gal-pals confided in him? I knew for a fact that Gabriel and Fancy had lunched together, though she knew he was my guy (at the time).

Oh, hell! So what was Gabriel going to say? I couldn't deny my sin, even if I wanted to. Harry had recharged my erotic batteries, and I simply looked it.

I'd consumed the entire split of champagne and was eyeing the jug of white wine when Barbara Evans walked in. "Tsk, tsk. Tell me something about it . . ." she said while rapidly filling up at the refreshment table.

I should have rolled my eyes and tried to blush, but I didn't. Maybe it wasn't too late. I held my breath—but damn it, my cheeks remained stone cold.

"Is it a new guy, Lizzie?"

I laughed bitterly. "Uh-huh."

"Are you going to have trouble talking about it?"

"It's new—I don't want to spoil it," I said hastily.

It had been wrong to be prompt tonight, particularly since I wanted to leave early, which was against the Austenian rule for proper etiquette. This conversation was less than five minutes old, and I wanted to run right out of here. I knew my pals wouldn't like the fact that Harry had replaced Gabriel with not so much as a thought. Too much like Lydia, Elizabeth's sister in *Pride and Prejudice.*

Just then, Gabriel returned, wearing an expensive black T-shirt torn across his chest at nipple level (I fear this was deliberate). Straining over his slim buttocks were the tightest shorts I'd ever seen. My angel looked sexy as hell. Still, I had to admit I was looking at him as a sex object, wasn't I?

Barbara grunted. Yes, I know it's unladylike, but that is what it sounded like. She was a Brunhilde, tall, blond, pale, and beautiful. Her preference was for short, squat, ethnic-looking men, but she'd break that for one shot with Gabriel—which he knew, and which he now obviously catered to.

"Hello, Babs." He gave her a peck on the cheek as his eyes searched mine out. I could see I'd hurt him dreadfully.

What's a girl to do? I adopted what I hoped was a hurt and victimized tone. "I am *so* sorry," I said.

Gabriel sent me a wrathful glance as Edgar Meredith walked in. With one sweeping glance, our mentor knew it was going to be a hot time.

"Ah, fireworks tonight. Good. I've had a boring day teaching students about nothing of importance." He smiled mischievously and added, "Now, who wants to start talking about something? And, my dears, let's all try for some Austenian irony, shall we?"

Chapter Three

— 1 —

A USTENIAN IRONY?

At our first session of JANO when we spoke about our Austen goals, I replied simply that I wanted to live in London and shag that darling lad with those sparkling blue eyes and *veree* naughty smile.

Everyone laughed at me when I said I was being ironic.

"That's bull. You're like the Red Queen in *Alice*—running, running with all these men while staying in the same place," Edgar remarked. "Rule 1: Please do not mention his name at any JANO meetings."

Having known me for a decade, he was all too aware of my obsession with the lad.

From that day on, objectified as a silly, simpering schoolgirl, I ignored most of the other members' names. In fact I completely blotted their entire personas, not the best approach for group communication.

So for the greater good I created a JANO scorecard for myself and other members.

Here goes:

Name	Fave Book	Fave Character	Personal Crisis
Babs	M. Park	Mary Crawford	Craves Gabe
Abigail	S&S	Marianne Dashwood	Sexual
Rick	Won't choose	Won't choose	Ex-priest
Rosalyn	P&P	Jane Bennet	Rick's nun
Natasha	M. Park	Fanny Price	Too rich
Bruce	P&P	Darcy	Method Actor
Dorothy	P&P	Lydia Bennet	Exotic dancer
Pauline	S&S	Elinor Dashwood	Hates heteros

Adding myself, Gabe, and Edgar adds up to eleven, but not everyone attended every meeting. Today, in fact, there were only five of us present—Babs, Abby, Gabe, Edgar, and myself.

We sat in a circle, then Edgar nodded to Abby to begin.

"I want to be a lesbian, you see," she said. "But I'm worried about what Jane Austen would say. Would she mind?"

"Well, she had all those ladies in *Emma* living together," Gabe said sharply. He was impatient to rat me out, so I had to think of ways to keep lesbianism as our topic.

"Yes," Abby looked worried. "But they were old maids, weren't they? Nowadays, lesbians aren't."

"That Miss Bates group gossiped quite a lot. And every gay person I know loves that," Babs added.

"That's a homophobic stereotype, not fit for JANO meetings," Edgar complained. "Both of you should be ashamed of yourselves."

Not to be silenced, Babs continued. "It has to do with vaginas, you see."

"Huh?" This from me.

Edgar's cheeks reddened, and his lips quivered as he digested this odd thought.

Babs cleared her throat. "According to my gynecologist, that darling twit Dr. Amos Sunshine, it seems there are two types of vaginas."

Gabe's eyes popped. "And they are???"

"There's the thin-skinned variety. Those are the ones that have frequent infections." While imparting this ultimately fascinating information, Babs rose from her chair and tackled the refreshment table. She returned, each hand holding a glass of Chablis.

"Is that why you're always going to see that Sunshine asshole?" Gabe snidely inquired.

Hmmm—odd remark. I didn't know Gabe and the tall gal spoke about such things.

In response, Babs bowed her head as if she were referring to a religious entity. Perhaps she was. "My vagina is quite sensitive and catches all sorts of germs."

"Oh?" I asked, not quite believing what I was hearing, but wanting to be supportive.

"And there's the other kind." Babs went on. "Awfully thick! I believe this is what distinguishes lesbians." Satisfied, she hurriedly downed both glasses of Chablis before stealing a scared look at Edgar.

She was right to worry. Was this an appropriate focus for our JANO meeting when our purpose was to discuss how to live civilly in a society devoted to sex, cell phones, and rock & roll?

"Let's get off this dreadful subject," Edgar admonished the group.

Appropriately chastised, Babs began wheezing, sneezing, choking, coughing, until she had to step out of the room. My suspicion—she was on her way to the lobby bar.

Quickly Gabe composed a new tune with lyrics about vaginas. He strummed an imaginary guitar, then gulped his blue flute of bubbly, trying to ignore the annoyed glances coming from our proper tea lady.

Oh, I forgot to mention, Abigail Moran was one of those Austen purists who insisted on tea . . .

– 2 –

WHEN JANO WAS ORGANIZED, we'd discussed what
would be served and decided not to do the tea thing—that
custom was entrenched among the academic groups. Besides,
at sixish, after working like a slave all day, who felt like tea?

Only Abby, who had the benefit of a lovely trust fund.
When she refused to give up this endearing custom of the
upper classes, we suggested that she bring her own tea things.
After all, we weren't fascists (at least not on the surface of
things).

Trying to negotiate a ceremonial tea at our meetings was
one of Abby's prime reasons for living. "There's simply
nothing like the elegance of tea," she'd announce each time.
"Come on, can't we have watercress, cucumber, and egg
salad sandwiches at our next meeting?"

"No way," Gabe always objected.

"How about caviar, blinis, prosciutto on ficelle, or hickory-
smoked turkey on carrot bread?"

"Shit, no." Gabe again.

Abigail was determined. Throughout this talk of thin and
thick vaginas, she cradled a Spode cup in both hands while
balancing a tray on her lap. It held a bowl of strawberries,
homemade scones, clotted cream, strawberry jam, and two
lace-trimmed linen napkins with the initials JA embroidered
on them, compliments of Abby's mum.

Abby sipped the tea appropriately, pinky out, holding the
saucer oh so delicately. Finished, she put the tray on the floor
next to a large basket. While the rest of us gave in to Gotham's
fast food items, Abby arrived complete with a *Sense and
Sensibility* basket—remember all the picnics in that book?

Gracefully, Abby examined her tea treats. The basket contained a small tin of Fortnum & Mason's New York Blend, which described its contents as "a fine leaf blend of superior quality Ceylon tea especially created for New York water!" Also a Royal Albert bone china teapot from England labeled "Enchantment," a mesh heart tea infuser bought locally which Abby sprayed with vibrant red gloss (*veree* un-British), and a tiny supply of Harrod's Lemon & Ginger Herbal Tea which Abby used as a chaser. She'd stopped at Brit Ltd. to pick up the clotted cream and strawberry jam from the UK.

Irritably, Gabe went back to the trenches. "Do you have a thin or thick vagina?" he asked her.

I could anticipate her reaction to his remarks. Yes, Abigail dropped her jaw, aghast at Gabriel's behavior. Ye gads!! That girlfriend was stubborn. You'd think after six months of this tea controversy, the gal would give up on any thoughts of her personal approach to Austen civility.

(You see, each one of us had our own version of an Austen life.)

"Oh, pleeease! I really don't think my private parts are a subject I want to discuss here," Abby said.

An odd thing to say, given the previous confessionals she'd shared with the group. After listening to Abby for the past six months, I'd come to the conclusion that she was sexually bored. She'd confided to us that she'd tried all kinds of sexual activity, traditional frontal, liberal anal, mouth-to-mouth, mouth-to-organ, leather costumes, pink frilly negligees, phone sex, silent sex, and (most shocking) she'd used clotted cream as a body aphrodisiac.

Though she certainly hadn't covered everything in the book of erotica, Abby had lately decided that she was beyond sexual happiness.

That's when she thought of turning gay.

— 3 —

AH, THIS IS WHY I LOVE Jane Austen. She seems like an elitist because she only writes about white people of a certain class, but she really isn't. People identify with different elements in her books, which is truly democratic in the long run.

Gabriel's identification with Austen was lusting over uncorseted ladies and hanging out with cigar-smoking gentlemen in a private club. Abigail's identification was ladies in hats and gloves who liked pink tablecloths and pink cake.

Both these Austenian elements left me feeling quite isolated, because I generally wore trainers, a sports bra, hi-cut briefs, and a running suit whenever I attended JANO.

Not today, though. My outfit consisted of velvet hip-hugger jeans, a low-cut silk top revealing nipple indentations, a lacy fringed shawl tied around my hips, and high-heeled snakeskin boots. I'd spent a half-hour blowing my long, dark hair so that it would look like Japanese cotton. But I resisted wearing heavy eye makeup, even though Harry told me he liked same.

— 4 —

THIS ENTIRE PACKAGE WAS AIMED at Harry's fantasies. I, for one, would have worn something much softer and feminine, but Harry had whispered in my ears that there was something about me that reminded him of Shania Twain (apparently his main turn-on). So wouldn't I do him a real fave whenever we had non-professional dinner dates like tonight? Wouldn't I wear that kind of garb?

I said no.

Harry said yes.

Then he added, "You have the kind of beauty that can carry off many different looks."

So I caved. But I was worried about what effect my wardrobe might have on the other JANO-ites.

Perhaps it was due to Gabe's darkened hotel room, but my sexy costume hadn't garnered too much disdain from Edgar.

Or maybe it was because the lesbian topic was more exciting?

Or maybe he knew my JANO secret . . .

You see, my identification with Austen was sexual, not literary. I wanted to make love to Darcy, Knightley—in fact, any Austen chap. So much so, that the men in my life really suffered in comparison.

I believed that Abby shared my sexual interest in those nineteenth century novels, though she covered it up with all this tea ceremonial bullshit. If my Darling Lad were in the near vicinity, I'd have to deck Abby fast—I'd wager she'd make a speedy run for him.

I wondered who would win. Me in my rock star garb or trust fund Abigail dressed to the nines in soft Italian leather slacks and jacket from Florence, Italy, topped with a bold silver necklace she'd purchased on her last trip to Mexico?

The thing was festooned with several silver ornaments which Abby explained were replicas of her lovers (male up to this point).

So there the lady sat, delicately pouring a second cup of tea as she talked about adopting a sexual preference as if it were a new pair of shoes.

"It's all so exciting," said she.

"So what's your problem?" Gabe prompted, still anxious to take the floor and crap on me.

"Thing is," Abby said *veree* much like Emma, "though I understand technically how to do it, I can't quite comprehend how to get excited without Mr. Dick bearing down on me."

"Mr. Dick?" I guffawed, unable to restrain myself.

"Yes, Mr. Dick. It's a really specific word. You know how we librarians love the language."

"Oh, yeah . . . librarians."

Abby had only worked as a librarian for two weeks, to prove to her wealthy father that she could hold down a job. She later explained that this experience was why she was careful with words, although what this had to do with her references to Mr. Dick, I don't know. Later when Abby called shagging "Señor Buck," I protested in my best feminist manner that the use of the masculine gender was sexist.

The truth is, I felt there were too many librarians in Austenland. Jane Austen groups needed more exotic dancers (we had one), shopgirls, waitresses . . . regular women, which didn't describe Abby at all.

Still, I had to admit that Abby had guts for bringing her musings out in the open. I'm sure every librarian has wondered what lesbians were like (not that there's anything wrong with that lifestyle). Librarians are no doubt curious types, and after reading all those repressed Bloomsbury novels where authors kept switching back and forth, who could blame them?

"Oh, fuck," Gabe said, rubbing his bare chest and swiveling his eyes to and fro in that sexy way he had. "That's not a problem. If you want to have a woman, just do it."

"Harrumph," Edgar cleared his throat. "Gabriel, let's have some compassion here. Abigail is baring her soul."

"More like boring," Gabe said, impatient for his turn at the wheel of Austenian logic.

I dunno. I couldn't see Gabe doing a gay turn during his childhood. Wouldn't his traditional family have stoned him? Gabe had to attend Harvard to learn that there were other options in life.

And I can't help wondering if I might have influenced him, too, by "cutting off his balls!!"

His phrase, not mine.

Oh, well!

All this introspection had made me rather ravenous for Harry. I picked up my backpack, made my excuses, bowing slightly to Edgar, and left.

− 5 −

BECAUSE I HAD A HOT DATE with Harry and hoped to have a sexually fulfilling night which might extend to the following day . . . and the next . . . I was laden down (don't you love those Britwords?) with a fully-equipped backpack:

1. ASPIRIN
2. SWISS ARMY KNIFE
3. A SEWING KIT, WITH 2 BUTTONS, THAT CALLS ITSELF A "MENDING KIT"—HOW OLD-FASHIONED—AS IF IT COULD MEND ANYTHING
4. TWO COLLAPSIBLE FOLDING CUPS, IN CASE THERE'S SOMETHING I WANT TO DRINK AND HAVE NOTHING TO DRINK FROM
5. A RAIN CAP—LIKE THE KIND LITTLE OLD LADIES PUT ON THEIR JUST-HAIRDRESSED COIFS WHEN A STORM COMES UP UNEXPECTEDLY

6. TOOTHPASTE/TOOTHBRUSH
7. A PAIR OF PANTIES—JUST IN CASE
8. PANTYHOSE
9. SHORT STOCKINGS, IN CASE I PASS A SHOE STORE
10. TAMPONS/PADS
11. A STRETCH WOOL HEADBAND TO COVER MY EARS
12. A PAD OF PAPER
13. A RED PEN
14. COUGH DROPS
15. GUM
16. TWO COPIES OF *EMMA*—JUST IN CASE
17. TWO BOXES OF STRAWBERRY FLAVORED CONDOMS
18. A VIBRATOR—JUST IN—OOPS!!

Often during a night of sex, I wake up in the middle of the night from dreams of running naked in the desert and use one of the essentials in my backpack. During these anxiety attacks I wonder what came before backpacks—the ultimate survival kit for those of us who explore Manhattan's sexual favors?

Of course, nothing could protect those Manhattan citizens who were in love.

Or were they?

You see, I believe there is no such thing as romance in Manhattan.

In this great city most people walk about in an invisible bubble, talking on their cell phones. In fact, one can't distinguish the crazies anymore. It used to be that when you heard someone talking to themselves, you could just move a certain distance away. Not anymore. Now everybody talks. No one is looking around . . . there is simply no flirting going on. Forget all those films.

Maybe I need a change of location. Remember Ralph Fiennes walking through the desert to save his love? Many women thought it was romantic, but when I watched that scene I drank so much Pellegrino that I had to go to the loo. Since I was at a private screening, this was truly embarrassing.

And remember the infamous scene with Bogart and Bergman in *Casablanca*? Well, Casablanca doesn't look like that anymore. So there!

It really doesn't matter, because romantic places do not turn me on. I simply like to be around gorgeous men who are comfortable about sex—those who don't turn it into "Am I the best fuck you've had?" or "Who was better than me?" or "Don't think this is a serious thing" or "See you later—call you next week" lies.

Still, in the middle of the night, when the world is quiet yet my heart is thumping so badly I can't sleep, I think that maybe this searching and carrying on isn't about sex.

Maybe that's only a ruse.

Maybe it's all about that illusory notion submerged by drugs, rock & roll, and those shoes that Sarah Jessica Parker wears on *Sex and the City*—just to name a few distractions.

Maybe it's really about L O V E ?

Or maybe it's about the white dress . . .

– 6 –

WHEN I READ THE JANE AUSTEN passage to my dad he looked puzzled. So I read it aloud again. "It is a truth universally acknowledged, that a single man in possession of a good fortune must be in want of a wife."

"Does this mean that Jane thinks every man should be married?" I asked.

He looked amused. "No, princess. She's more or less saying that at that time women had to marry men of property."

"Why?" My nine-year-old eyes widened.

"Women didn't have many choices then," he explained somberly. "But you're lucky. You never have to marry if you don't want to."

"But I want to be in love . . . and . . ."

"There are many different ways to love, Lizzie. It doesn't have to be traditional."

"Traditional?"

"You know, a white dress, a church . . ."

"Mom doesn't have a white dress."

"Yes, I know."

"Did you get married in a church?"

"I'll tell you the whole story some day."

But he never did.

Chapter Four

— 1 —

THERE WERE PINK DRINKS everywhere, typical for film launch parties. But replacing the usual buffet—ripening cheeses, pates, huge shrimps, Asian food, strawberries, and every kind of cracker invented—were tables laden with computer games, toys, comic books (the fat ones called graphic novels), action figures, costumes, and a collection of weapons—the special-effects merchandising of a comic book film.

I knew little about comic books (in my adolescence I read *Seventeen* magazine and Jane Austen novels), but I had a minor interest in this phenomenon. Two years ago, I'd written an essay for a women's magazine discussing how buddy films were out and wondering what the boys in Hollywood would think of next. Here was the answer: comic book heroes.

It was six P.M., and everyone was headed towards the lobby bar because drinking was part of the job. For media types, drinking isn't just a pleasant outing, it's a way to organize our work life. When my colleagues and I get down and dirty, too many admit we drank more than we shagged.

Personally, I tried hard to stay healthy through

Pellegrino consumption. Because I was a freelancer, I could get away with this.

My daily schedule:

7 A.M.–9 A.M.
Wake-up time. Coffee and bagels while watching morning shows for tidbits about stars—unless I'd gotten lucky and slept with a cutie. In that case, put on a tape and shag instead.

9 A.M.–11 A.M.
Phone calls to New York editors, agents, public-relations people, before they went out to lunch. First Pellegrino.

11 A.M.–2 P.M.
Write copy, unless I had a business lunch date or a noon-spin with same cutie.

2 P.M.
All coast calls ... tracking down stars and/or their entourages on film sets. Lying. Bargaining for news. Sometimes threatening, or more honestly, blackmailing them. Second Pellegrino.

4 P.M.
Check calendar, bathe, dress.

5 P.M.
Night activities, i.e. JANO meeting, a launch party, a film preview, hopefully a pickup. Several Pellegrinos.

9 P.M.
When dated up, like tonight, I log into my adventurous, young-at-heart mode, switch to liquor, and hope these pink things won't alter my erotic high. Also wish the same for my date. Swilling it down has caused many men to lose their ... you know.

Tonight was going to be fine. The good news was that Harry could hold his liquor and stay quite firm as well.

ↀↀ

As the crowd surged bar-ward, I lurked beside the ladies' room door, where Tony Palermo spotted me. His eyes opened wide in shock as he removed his right hand from the buttocks of a blonde.

"What the *hell*, Lizzie! Are you in costume?"

"Didn't have time to change."

That was the absolute truth. I'd thought I was going to meet Harry Archer at a low-class bar—maybe Suzy's on East Fifth Street—a haunt with a jukebox, a pool table, and lots of thuggish types with spiky blond hair running around in tight pants plus low-cut shirts.

I'd even invented a scenario where I would walk in and pretend not to know Harry. I'd walk up and down the bar, eyeing the thug-guys, then wave them away like dominos and go up to Harry. Boy, that would turn him on, wouldn't it?

All day long I wondered what Harry would wear. Would he wear all black, one of those wonderful black sweaters that hug his chest, those expensive tailored trousers, and trainers? Sexy as hell.

But my fantasies changed when I left the JANO meeting. That's when Babs caught me in the hotel lobby, blabbering about how she wanted to shag Gabriel and would I mind now that I had another guy.

Before I could answer, my cell phone rang. It was Harry's assistant, a smallish, thinnish, tinyish girl named Heather who wore a skirt up to her ass and high high heels, hoping that both would interest my Harry.

"Mr. Archer asked that you meet him at *The Fist* launch. He said to get there before six."

"Ugh!"

I'd already turned down my invitation to that film launch. Three times the film had been ready to go, only to be canceled. When an independent company put in eight million, it was later killed by a number-crunching studio. Finally, everyone involved agreed to make it as a cheaper digital film.

Did I want to see this crap? Not really. So I responded, "Sorry, I'll be out of town." Now the publicist would know I'd been lying through my teeth. I had an excuse ready, simply telling her I had a change of plans. (I must remember I'm a film critic, not a goddamn publicist. I'm important!)

I asked sleazy Heather, "Are you sure about this?" I noted my voice had become *veree* sharp.

"I'm sure."

Bang. Hang up.

I checked my wristwatch. It was five-thirty. Was Harry serious? He'd asked me to dress like this and wanted me to appear at a launch with all my professional peers.

I dialed his private number. No answer.

Hell! This is what happens when you shag the boss. I couldn't refuse. It was an order.

I ran out of the hotel and hailed a cab. Apparently, my outfit was working—the driver began to sing in Spanish.

"Could you cool it?" I said as he ogled me in the rear-view mirror.

"You are *muy bonita!*"

I replied in the Queen's English. "Please keep your eyes on the *bloody* road."

Back to Tony's question. "Why are you dressed like that?"

"I thought this was a motorcycle film launch, and this would be appropriate."

"Lizzie, that's bull. What's it about?"

I grabbed his T-shirt to pull him close. "I've a hot date with Harry, and he asked me to wear this outfit."

Tony gave me an odd look. "You have a date with Harry?"

"You know we've been at it."

Tony's deep Italian eyes filled with moisture, so I knew the news was bad. Just then Fancy strolled by, her inky-black hair twisted back into a tight bun, her onyx eyes and tawny skin conveying a sense of mystery—though her little cropped sequin sweater revealed most of her breasts.

"Have you been sniffing?" She rolled her eyes, though she knew I wasn't one of those.

"Lizzie has a date with Harry, and he asked her to wear this outfit," Tony said in a peculiarly *La Boheme* tone of voice.

"A date with Harry!!" Now Fancy was doing it, too.

"Hey, what's with you two? You know Harry and I have been shagging."

"Lizzie . . ." Fancy began. Then she drew a sharp breath and muttered, "Oh, no."

I turned to check what had startled my girlfriend. It was Harry, dressed to the nines in a dark suit, dark shirt open at the throat, no jewelry. Spotting me, his intense eyes roved me up and down as he nodded approval like a damned procurer.

On his arm, whispering in the ear that I had nuzzled only this morning, was Sherry McBride, the young star of *Fabulous* which I'd reviewed with great enthusiasm only last week. Well, that would change!

"I'm going to kill him," I said between set teeth.

But, as I began my kick-boxing routine, Fancy whispered our mantra.

"*Don't Be The Girl!*" she said.

— 2 —

SLOWLY I UNCLENCHED MY FISTS, though continuing to gnash my teeth. Tony took hold of both my arms, twisted his hands around mine, and whispered, "Let's get out of here. Fresh air will help."

With Fancy on one side and Tony on the other, we pushed through the fatuous crowd. "Hey, Lizzie," someone called.

"It's all right, Lizzie. I'll wave." Tony did, then said to Fancy, "She's terribly pale. She might faint. Should we take her to the hospital?"

Fancy muttered, "Let's just walk." As she stooped to remove her spike-heeled boots, she inadvertently mooned the paparazzi. They swarmed around us, but realizing we were media, went back to hounding the celebs. In a quick trot, Fancy and Tony walked me down to the Red Lion Lounge, a place I wouldn't generally be seen dead in. We walked to the back through neon-lit darkness (who hung out here, anyway?) and told the frizzy-haired waitress that we wanted Pellegrino.

She shrugged. "Only got club soda."

That did it. I burst into tears. I kept wailing away in front of Fancy and Tony's astonished faces. They tried to console me, but I was blubbering about another time, another place.

"You're a silly girl," Mom said. "You have everything to live for. Don't waste your time being a crybaby."

When I wouldn't stop, she added, "You're Daddy's little princess, aren't you?"

Was that awful to be?

I liked being Daddy's princess, because he hugged and kissed me and told me things were all right.

But Mom didn't believe in coddling me, especially when I cried. Instead, Mom told me I was a silly, stupid girl.

All my life I wondered if she was right.

"I'm sorry," I apologized to my pals between sniffles.

"Hey, if it helps, do it," Fancy said.

"Here, use my handkerchief." Like any Italian man living at home, Tony was always armed with a lovely linen handkerchief, cleaned and pressed by Momma.

"I'll mess it up," I whimpered.

"Then mess it up. But don't mess up that pretty face of yours."

Then Tony reached out to hold my hand.

Oh, sometimes men were the *best* people.

I calmed down a bit when the fizz arrived. That's when Tony asked Fancy, "What did you mean—don't be the girl?"

"It's our mantra," Fancy replied, checking to see if I was back to normal. I was.

"Huh?" This from Tony.

"You see, we're the generation of women who can do ANY FUCKIN' THING WE WANT! But when it comes to men—WE HAVE TO BE THE GIRL! Men don't like it when we aren't. We have to be thin, have perfect hair, wear tons of makeup, buy expensive, killer high heels and silky outfits to wear even though it's freezing, know how to cook, discuss Shakespeare, watch football, go mountain-climbing . . . shall I go on?"

Two ughs from me. I was back on track.

Fancy smiled. "So Lizzie and I came up with a sensational mantra: *Don't Be The Girl.*"

"That's cool. But explain—if you were going to be the girl, what would you have done?"

Fancy responded. "She was about to create an *Othello* tableau."

"Othello?"

I jumped in. "I was about to pop that damn Harry right in the bazooka . . . if you know what I mean. Then smack that Sherry chick on her cosmetically-altered nose."

"Sherry may have nothing to do with it," Fancy said cautiously. "Remember, girls hating girls is what guys want us to do." She nodded sympathetically. "Of course if you were a public item, if you were Harry's wife or something, then you could rearrange Sherry's fake face without needing real evidence. But under the circumstances, with you and Harry shagging in secret, you can't blame her."

"You are too wise." Tony nodded in agreement.

"Don't worry about that Sherry bitch," I said. "I'll take care of her in print."

Fancy frowned. "Lizzie, you're supposed to be totally unbiased in your film reviews." She took a sip of the fizzy stuff, licked her full lips, and added, "I don't think Harry will let you get away with knocking people just because he likes them."

"I don't know if I'll have a job with Horrid Harry—once I do the thing."

"The thing?" Now Tony looked scared. "And what would that be?"

"What would *you* do in the same circumstances?"

He thought for a moment. "I'd probably want to pound the guy who was dipping into my lady. But if I really wanted to hurt *her*? I'd call her best friend and ask her out. Then my lady would grovel."

"And be the girl," Fancy interjected.

"Hey, you're right. She'd yell and scream at me, but I'd have the advantage." Tony looked at me admiringly. "So you're going to get some guy and shove him in Harry's face?"

"Not just some guy. A hunk!" I said, savoring my imminent revenge.

Fancy knew immediately. "You mean gorgeous Gabriel?"

Yes, I had to make serious plans to seduce Gabe again, all the while knowing that I'd probably have to pay big for this wicked deed. Using people was not popular at JANO.

But as I read *Emma*, Jane Austen wasn't entirely against manipulation.

Was she?

– 3 –

THE NEXT MORNING I WOKE UP with major head pain, so I immediately went to the computer and my reality file:
Excuses I Know Are Lies.
I typed quickly.
Harry could have called and said:
"Something came up at the last moment."
Or:
"Sorry, I can't make it."
Then—
I wouldn't walk into that damned theater and look like an idiot.

I was pissed off.
I was even more pissed off after an hour passed.
Hey, what are cell phones for?
But suppose he simply forgot?
Do I let him off the hook?
Do I cut him a little slack?
But he was out with someone else!
No, that was too annoying.

He'd have to grovel.
Fitting punishment, if he didn't have the decency to let me know.
If he didn't want to keep our date, why didn't he try to reach me and tell me?
Why was he so vague, having that tart Heather tell me to show without details?
He knew I was dressed like a damn whore.

Ohmigod!

Is he trying to ruin me?

Is he trying to make me the laughingstock of the New York Media?

Has he told everyone we've shagged?

Did he say I was good in bed?

Hot?

Or boring?

Oh, God . . .

WHY DID I SHAG THE BOSS!!!!!

With heavy heart, I lay down on my pink velvet couch and wept bitterly. After an hour, I decided this response was way out of line. I had to cheer myself up. I turned on the computer again to read the London headlines.

There *he* was—my Darling Lad, frolicking at a chic club. No doubt he wasn't alone. I burst into violent tears. Why had I been cursed with this terrible crush on a man everybody else wanted to shag? Even if I got the opportunity, I wouldn't have the nerve. I was smart enough to know that my fantasies were not reality.

In the midst of this frustration, my cell phone rang. "Lizzie, here." I noticed my voice was *veree* throaty from sexual excitement.

Harry growled, "You don't sound as if you're alone."

"Is this a business call?" I tried to switch gears from sex to revenge.

"Lizzie, I know you're sore about last night, but I had to take Sherry out to dinner. We're doing a major story on her. Ron couldn't do it, so I had to fill in."

"Since when does your boss, Ronald Eldridge, with six kids, five dogs, and a possessive wife, take actresses out to dinner?"

"N-normally, never," Harry stammered, "but Ron has a major crush on Sherry. He's out of his mind about her, and he's risking everything."

"Does he know she has fake tits?"

"I'm not sure about that," Harry taunted.

"You've done the research?"

"Sherry positively threw herself at me. I had to act like a gentleman."

"Does that mean you shagged her?"

His voice got strange. "Not exactly."

"Exactly what?" Cripes, I was sounding like his wife! Must change that.

"Don't know whether I should tell you this under the circumstances."

"What circumstances? Because we spent some time in my bed? Don't worry, old sport. It was simply fun."

"*Fun!!!*" From the way he was suddenly hyperventilating, I thought he'd have a heart attack.

"Are you okay?"

He choked, took a deep breath, and growled again.

Fine. No mercy needed.

"Harry. We have a professional relationship. I write film reviews for your publication and, on occasion, shag you."

"On occasion? Hell, I thought we were going somewhere with this." Harry's voice got vehement.

Don't Be The Girl. Don't Be The Girl. I wasn't going to forget my mantra.

"Lizzie, we have to have a talk. I'm coming over there later."

"Don't do that, Harry."

"Be there about six."

He slammed the phone down.

– 4 –

OKAY, WHAT TO DO? I conferred with Fancy, who told me this was really tricky. "You could lose your gig," she warned. "How important is this to you?"

"I have to maintain my dignity. No man is going to fuck me over."

"Okay, then go to the next phase. If you want revenge, jealousy is the path. When Harry arrives, make sure you have the hunk around. That'll do Harry in."

"Fine."

"Good luck," Fancy said.

I went to my refrigerator and checked the champagne stock. Yes, there was a bottle handy. I ran to my wardrobe and plucked a lovely silk see-thru robe, slippers, tiny undies. Clad for sex, I dialed Gabe. But halfway through his number, I stopped. What I was doing was silly, silly, silly. Was this proper behavior for a Jane Austen disciple? No. I would simply be honest with Harry. I'd tell him that all this puckering about fucking wasn't for me. I was an ardent type who took my shagging seriously.

I called Fancy again and told her my decision. "Let me remind you," she said sternly, "Don't Be The Girl. Don't be soft and sweet. Don't be pliable. Keep up a strong front. And never say yes."

"Why?"

"Because no is shorter."

"What else?"

"Never be docile."

"You said that already."

"This time it's different. Always be independent. Be cool."

"Tell you the truth, Fancy-lady, I'm tired of being super-cool."

"And why is that?"

"Because it's getting me nowhere fast. It's getting all of us nowhere. We're simply not finding lovely, romantic men. All we have are guys we negotiate with."

"Remember, Lizabeth, you're not married to Harry, so we're not really going against Jane Austen's morality rules. You don't have to be truthful."

"You want me to grab the hunk and shag him. But I have a problem. First, is this fair to Gabe? And second, I don't know how to cheat. I've never dared."

"Ohmigod!" Fancy moaned. "You're quite the infant."

Hell!

"You're going to have to bite the bullet and do it!" Fancy admonished sternly, then took another call.

I felt my whole life was a joke. Here I was, going on and on about which films were good and which were ghastly, writing a screenplay about love and sex and life, debating whether or not to shag Harry again, whispering the mantra of *Don't Be The Girl*, and most of all insisting that my Darling Lad is perfect and would turn my life into a continual erotic high . . . and in his absence knowing that true love was pathetic.

It was ironic in a Jane Austen sort of way. I was about to be cited at JANO by Gabriel for switching from him to Harry, when the truth was . . .

I don't know how to cheat.

I've never been able to shag more than one man at a time.

Okay, sometimes it was really close—like shagging Gabe during the week and starting with Harry on the weekend—but there was never an overlap.

NO.

NEVER.

Still, I had to try.

Chapter Five

— 1 —

MY PROBLEM WAS THAT too many men had cheated on me, and I couldn't return the gesture. Call me a coward, call me socially inept, but I remember how I felt . . . each time it happened.

The first time, I was dreaming about Prince Charming on a white horse rescuing me from living with Mom and Dad. At the time, I was in love with Billy De Luca and *veree* jealous of the fact that he liked Mary Murphy better than me.

Mom told me to treat Billy as if he didn't exist.

It worked. Billy asked me to his birthday party—with the seating plan putting me right next to the birthday boy. After he blew out the candles, he whispered that I was pretty and suggested we go into the hall so I could unbutton my blouse. I refused, so he changed chairs and sat next to MM.

When I told Mom, she said that men were crap, but they were the only thing we non-lesbians had to love and that we had to put up with their constant need for sexual excitement and adventure from every new woman who came down the pike.

"Is there any hope at all?" I asked.

She shook her head. "Just remember, never bow and get on

your knees before a man, because he will go from you in your adoring position and crave the next pretty woman he sees."

(At the time Dad was working for Sam Shapiro, the legendary producer. Rumor had it that every lady at Shapiro Films was do-able. No wonder Mom was bitter.)

"So all men are cheats?" I quizzed.

That's when Mom told me Dad was moving out.

Dad simply disappeared. I couldn't understand why. All the other kids who had parents split saw both their dads and moms.

When I asked Mom, she refused to talk about it.

"But maybe something's wrong with him," I persisted. "Maybe he's hurt or ill. What if he needs us?"

When she answered, her voice was icy-cold. "I don't know where he is, Lizzie. And I don't care."

I didn't believe her for one minute. I knew that Mom was driven . . . and was terrified of failure. And she'd failed with Dad, hadn't she?

After that, we didn't talk about Dad.

And—as the years passed and I entered the world of dating—I began to understand Mom's pain.

I began college with the realization that my formal education would take four years, but my life as a woman would go on until my death. That's when I decided to concentrate on the latter.

Through my first year I read a lot of literary novels whose heroines were slightly mad: Anna Karenina, Madame Bovary, Lady Brett Ashley: those women with wild-eyed looks and uninhibited boudoir behavior were punished. Not for me. I tried to look wan, pale, ethereal, and shy. Joel

Parker was smitten and stayed that way until one day I expressed a *veree* vocal opinion about football. That's when Joel took off with Amelia Smiley.

Sophomore year I played female Casanova, utterly flirtatious. No frat boy could pin me down. I'd say yes to Dave, then no. I'd say I was truly in love with Allan, then tell him that I was engaged to Dave. This silliness went back and forth until both beaus started sniffing at Mary Murphy's feet. (Yes, the same MM I lost Billy De Luca to.)

For my third year I was more romantic, dating Charley, whose apartment was piled with pizza boxes and dirty bed linen. I wanted an egalitarian relationship. This meant I paid my own checks and insisted on having equal orgasms. That's when I learned that orgasms are unequal (girls simply have more!) I guess Charley got jealous of my frequent flying, because I found him in bed with a freshman known to be a virgin.

In my senior year, I was celibate.

When I joined the workforce, I met Manhattan bachelor types (I called them He-Men). They were shallow, self-involved, cynical, suffering from commitment phobia, and quite frankly, into charming the pants off every girl in the room. These were single men with few family ties, heavy career responsibilities, and healthy bank balances.

Harvey, my personal He-Man, loved his technology, electronic toys, trainer shoes, and could be taken for a gay fashion type due to his visits to hair salons, gyms, spas, and the like. I was happy to be Harvey's girl. But on the nights I went to the library, my He-Man cheated.

When caught, he explained that there were girl gangs in every chic bar, as well as girl-packs at sports events. They were healthy, good-looking women. Could he resist? Harvey explained that girls like me—who lead busy, glamorous lives—are disposable. Apparently, I was only an item in our consumer culture where negotiations and renewables were the norm.

In my suffering, I searched for wounded types. I called them Wu-Men. These used-up men were plentiful. Wu-men were divorced, or men who'd never had a relationship. My personal Wu-man was Bradley. He had strange fetishes, none of which included reading Jane Austen. Later I learned that Bradley was still seeing the ex-wife who'd wounded him.

That's my dating history, and I'm afraid it's not a happy one. My life has been filled with cheating men. (Is there any other kind?)

I was staring thirty-three in the face, and in a flash I'd be pushing forty. Tragic. I knew it. Fancy knew it. And Bridget Jones certainly knew it.

My exciting life as a film critic, with a network of glam pals; the gorgeous hunks I might possibly shag; the serious life topics at JANO . . . all these could not change the fact that I was still single.

My value in the marketplace had already declined. Harry's damn Heather was twenty-six and already contemplating a face-lift. That chippie was smarter than I was. She didn't waste any time—just aimed straight for the bosses. While Harry Archer was single, Ronald Eldridge was not. But young Heather didn't give a thought to behaving properly—she knew that MEN LOVED TO CHEAT.

I was on the losing side. While it's true that Jane Austen taught me how to ignore men, cheating was undignified for any Austen Girl. In Gotham, this meant I had a handicap.

Here, all sex is a marketplace.

Everyone wants to do it with everybody, and no one wants to pay the penalty.

— 2 —

I WAS A TOTAL DISASTER when suddenly, the best two months of my life happened! I met two men who read Jane Austen, had plentiful incomes, had never married, and lived in great apartments.

I shagged both of them—sequentially!!!

Now came the hard part. I had to keep one of them hot and heavy for me, and the only way to do that was to play the jealousy card.

Harry had the charisma which comes from having a terrific job with power—and having a terrific torso. He was also qualified in the stud area—*veree* terrific in the sack. Accordingly, to cheat on Harry meant I'd have to choose someone superior. Did Gabriel have the qualifications to usurp Harry? True, he had money, a gorgeous torso, and read Jane Austen. But Gabe didn't have a power job, though one might think that his inherited wealth would substitute for that. And Gabe wanted me—*veree* important!!

Okay. Must make a decision on my next move. Harry is coming over and will probably demand sex and love. Did I want to go back to shagging Gabe to screw Harry's head? And did I want to do that right now so that Gabe and I would be intertwined when Harry rang the bell?

If I'm in Gabe's arms, what happens? I had all sorts of scenarios. Harry might stomp out. Or he could toss Gabe out, lock the door, and try to seduce me. Of course, Gabe could pound on the door and perhaps break back in. Or maybe Gabe would use one of his tricks (oddly, he could open locks with a credit card), re-enter my boudoir, and then pound on Harry.

All *veree* violent—which did not turn me on.

Perhaps I'd be truly Jane Austen, untangle Gabe's arms from around my torso, and ask if they'd like a cup of tea.

Uh-uh. Too British.

Perhaps if they got ugly, I'd order both men to leave. Then Gabe would probably phone to call me a bitch of the ball-breaking variety. Gabe is totally unable to face competition because he never had to—never having had a job.

Maybe Harry would come by later holding candy, flowers, and a Tiffany box, which would earn him immediate erectile pleasure, compliments of yours truly. How easily my virtue is bought!

I could chuck this "cheater" idea and be a lady, maintaining my Jane Austen code of conduct whilst Harry tried to talk me back into the sack (and whilst I tried to ignore the bulge in his trousers).

It's important to remember that in Jane Austen novels, swathes of beautiful clothing protected ladies from male erectile excitement. Also, ladies insisted on being called Miss or Madam and expected men to rise (did this have a sexual connotation?) when they came into a room. Most importantly, ladies never had sex until wedded. (Well, we know that's changed!!!)

Problem is, if I marry, I won't have a chance with my Darling Lad . . . because whereas another girl could lie and flirt, though married, an Austen Girl simply cannot.

– 3 –

OH GOD! SEX AND ROMANCE have become depressingly demystified by obsessively analytical critics like myself. I've come to the conclusion that though I want it all—I DON'T KNOW WHAT IT IS I WANT!

Dating in Gotham is a set of games with new rules—but we get mixed signals, because it's open season on sex. And absolutely no one seems to know the right moves. With sex a common occurrence, things just go haywire.

Cheating doesn't really help. Besides, it's a huge amount of work. It's hard enough to track one guy—when does he call, does he arrive on time, how is he in the sack, is he sexy, kind, adorable, interesting, and can he pay the check? All this takes an interminable amount of thinking, planning, and recording.

In desperation, I've come up with a few simple rules:

Never show a guy you really like him, or he'll crap all over you.
Never say yes too fast, though he begs and says he wants you veree much.
Always have a secret, safe man that no one knows about—a man who listens to you.
Always have condoms in your purse.

— 4 —

BEFORE I COULD DO ANYTHING about Harry's expected arrival, Sam Shapiro phoned. Recently my dad's old boss had been profiled in several magazine articles and classy television interviews as a mogul in decline. Former colleagues kept accusing Sam of hustling them out of profits. Too many creative types claimed Sam never let them finish films according to the approved screenplay. Rumor had it that Sam would arrive on the set a week before the wrap to tell these auteurs how he wanted the ending changed, and to do it fast and cheap.

This wasn't news. When Dad worked for Sam, the same stuff was happening. Though sued, slammed, and shunned by most in the industry, Sam's tiny film studio had steadily grown throughout the Eighties and Nineties until today it was considered the equal of all those West Coast titans.

Though he was blunt and stupid and cheap, Sam loved good films. And despite being in the last season of his life, he never stopped fighting for what he believed to be cinematic truth.

I admired Sam for sticking to his guns but wasn't one of his fans. Mostly because Sam always tried to bribe critics—in fact, his finagling had gotten some of them fired.

Sam was a busy man, so a phone call from him meant that something was really important. Aside from running his now-huge studio, Sam had seven kids, thirty-five grandkids, and was famous as a family man—though also quite infamous as a cheater.

The mogul's raspy voice sounded grimmer than usual. "Look, kiddo, I'm doing you a favor."

This was trouble.

"Sorry, Sam, I can't take gratuities."

He hissed ominously. "It's not that kind of favor."

"What other kind is there?"

"It's personal."

I waited in wonder. What could Sam Shapiro have on my personal life? Had my shagging Harry gone public? If yes, maybe I could ask Sam how to be a cheater.

Suddenly my heart flipped. Could Sam know something of my father's whereabouts?

Then he said, "I was up at the Spring Festival, and some sleazebag is getting a lot of attention with his documentary."

Ah! This was a professional call. "An indie?"

"Absolutely. He's using footage from the Sixties."

The ends of my hair started to curl, but I was *tres* cool.

"I'll see it when you screen it."

"Look, kiddo, I like you. That's why I'm making this really personal call."

"You can't bribe me, Sam."

"What bribe? You're family. I've known you since you were a cute kid."

"Okay, so what's up?"

"Well—there's a lot of broads running around in the buff—"

Disaster.

Mom taught me that whenever a crisis looms, asking a rhetorical feminist question is wise.

"Is there any artistic or political value to the nudity?"

"Naw. It'll help sell tickets."

Try Edgar's rules and regulations now: "Anything of a romantic nature?"

Sam sounded tired. "Gimme a break."

Okay—switch to my journalistic sharp technique. "Are you saying that this indie film is porno?"

He was careful—too careful. "Not exactly."

"So what are you saying about the film?"

"I'm not talking about the film, Lizzie! I'm talking about the star of the scene!!"

My literary ears perked up. I wanted to shout, *stop screwing around, Sam, give it to me.* Obviously it was really good gossip.

But I kept cool. "The star? Someone famous?"

"Wrong. Wrong. Wrong."

I added, "Perhaps a romantic icon? A Doris Day type? A Miss Goody-two-shoes?"

"This, too, will pass," Sam muttered.

"Then who?" I waited.

"Lizzie, dahling, the main babe with the bouncing boobs and the curly hot twat is your Mom."

Chapter Six

— 1 —

ARRY ARCHER KEPT TRYING to enter my dream—cute, adorable Harry kept blowing kisses. When that didn't work, he began to disrobe until I had real evidence of his desire staring me in the face.

Oh, no!

My subconscious was in turmoil. I didn't want Harry there, because my Darling Lad was in permanent residence. He was comfortably one step removed from my celluloid-wrapped heart (though I hoped to meet him in the future), whereas Harry was all flesh and blood and erection.

I woke up with a start. Sprawled on my couch, I fell into a deep depression. That can happen when an underpinning of your life suddenly evaporates. I had an image from Botticelli's painting of Venus, her hair flowing in the wind, girlfriends around her, all standing on a delicate seashell which is about to crack.

We're silly sea nymphs swimming in the deep, dark waters of sex, searching for men of grace.

Do we know what we are doing?

I don't think so.

I went to the fridge and sought out my chocolate stash.

(Bridget really knew what she was talking about!) Hidden in the snack drawer were three Perugina dark chocolate bars, which took about two seconds to disappear as I stared out the window, watching boats sail up and down the Hudson River. (Yes, I have a river view—eat your heart out.)

But all that serenity and beauty repelled me. My headache was getting worse as Sam Shapiro's vulgar words haunted me. *My Mom in a nudie film!!!*

What reason could she possibly have? The feminist refrain from the Sixties was "burn your bra!" Hmmm—but that certainly didn't translate to *bare your twat!!!*

Maybe Mom had a hidden sexual agenda that I didn't know about. As far as I knew, she flirted and probably had affairs with men after dad left. But Mom was very secretive, almost CIA-like, about this kind of thing, all the while telling me that sexuality was good as long as the man didn't dictate the action.

"Women have sexual needs," Mom said whilst munching on her special goat cheese and spinach ravioli. Her mouth was covered with the white stuff, so she looked a little like those strangely erotic silent film stars. (Who did their makeup, for heaven's sake?)

I was enthralled with Billy De Luca at the time and had only gotten as far as fantasizing about kissing him—and here Mom was talking about sexual needs?

"Mom, what does that mean? Should I let Billy—I mean if I can ever interest him—?"

She opened her mouth wide, revealing spinach leaves stuck between her fine white teeth. "Don't you dare . . . wait until you absolutely, *really* want someone, and then talk to me."

Of course, I didn't.

Like other feminist mothers, Mom had a set of rules politically, but when it came to her baby girl—hands off!

Oh, stop thinking about the past, Lizzie! You're thirty-
three years old, for heaven's sake.

Act like it.

I tried. Gooey and trashed out, I searched for potato chips.
There were none. I'd have to visit the corner gourmet shop
where chips came in gold foil bags boasting absolutely no fat.
(I might add, no taste either.)

Maybe I'd also pop into the video rental shop and roam
about the UK section. Perhaps there'd be a guy with a British
accent and a razor-sharp wit.

Or maybe I'd hang at the mystery bookstore, where I
might meet a stranger wearing a wide fedora (which meant
he's from San Francisco). Maybe he'd take his hand out of
his raincoat pocket (where I assume he had a gat) to pene-
trate my disguise.

For this fantasy I'd have to change. My scotch plaid pajama bottoms and white hi-cut panties were not sexy enough
for a stranger's touch. I thought of going commando, but
decided that was really unsanitary. But if you want to make
sparks, there has to be a little friction and risk-taking.

(I believe sincerely that one should never come across as
benign while having a fantasy).

Inside my undies drawer were boxers, boxer briefs, and
bikinis. I slipped on a red bikini but not the matching bra. I'd
go bare under my T-shirt with the words PIECE, NOT WAR
printed on the chest. (No, I don't think it's a misspelling.)

I didn't feel like doing the "face." If I wore enormous
Nautica sunglasses and Hard Candy lip gloss, I'd look decent,
wouldn't I? Like Garbo, I'd move in the shadows, a woman of
mysterious sensuality.

In the kitchen, I tossed garbage into proper plastic green bags (the NYPD arrested New Yorkers for less). Might as well do the whole job. From the refrigerator I tossed out the creepy brussels sprouts, the wilted broccoli, and a piece of brie that stank up the whole room. I wrapped the bags tightly and kicked them down the hall towards the door.

Hmmm. Why was I so angry?

Maybe because Harry hadn't sent me twenty pink tulips with a card saying he was sorry. Or Gabriel calling me a ball-breaker. Or maybe because of Mom. She always said that we had a wonderful relationship, that we were honest with each other even when the truth was going to cause problems.

Then why hadn't I ever heard about Mom's nude film? She knew I wasn't a prude. I'd been told all about Gran's scandalous life—everyone knew about the infamous Alice Parsons.

I picked up Gran's photograph in the silver frame and kissed her forehead. Alice always said that whenever things got bad, do something silly. She was right. I felt hurt and disappointed. If I didn't do something stupid, I would probably just bawl my eyes out.

– 2 –

AS FATE WOULD HAVE IT, the fax machine began churning. My special article on how film stars were treated in the tabloids had been marked up by the boss, my famously hands-on editor (in more ways than I'd like to deal with right now).

The title was *Body Fascism*. I'd focused on body shapes of actresses who suffered from eating disorders or had conspicuous cosmetic surgery, citing the frantic demands of producers and directors who required "perfect" bodies as the ones responsible for this sadistic behavior.

In the margin, Harry had added in a large, emphatic scrawl: "Are men the enemy? Don't most women like to bitch about their bodies—and their girlfriends'?"

I blanched at Harry's notations, but that wasn't what shot me over the edge. Now my article was accompanied by paparazzi shots of well-known actresses in bikinis, taken in the privacy of their Malibu beach houses. Alongside were touched-up publicity shots of these stars. *Veree* different.

On one, Harry had written a postscript. "Like your bod with or without a bikini!"

I was furious but also confused. *The Village Record* had a huge female audience and often published articles about their issues. In my cinema reviews, Harry gave me no problem about my bias for women's films. But now the long arm of Harry's fury (though he was the guilty one, wasn't he?) was corrupting my article.

I had no recourse, the editor-in-chief had the last say. But I was steaming. I had to come up with a plan. (I'm ashamed to admit that I planned to use my newfound position as Harry's babe for career advantage.)

So I wrote on the fax, "This is not acceptable, let's discuss in *detail*."

I was about to re-fax when I realized it was evidence. If I ever wanted to take Harry Archer to sexual harassment court (wherever that is), his notation about my bod was proof that he was getting a bit too personal. My hands shook as I pondered what to do. I must confess, I almost decided to forget about it.

But something my grandmother taught me made me stop and think. "Always have something in the safe-deposit box," Alice advised. "Something to save your ass when you need it."

Quickly, I wrote my comments on a notepad. Then I faxed

the note and saved Harry's fax. But I felt guilty, guilty, guilty. Getting evidence on Harry, who I really wanted and who hadn't had to persuade me, didn't seem like proper sexual harassment. Besides, would Harry understand what I meant by "discuss in detail?" It was an obvious invitation for sex, wasn't it?

Oh dear! Wouldn't my comments be evidence for Harry if he ever wanted to take *me* to sexual harassment court!

If anyone asked me officially, I'd have to say yes. But wasn't Harry sexually harassing me by mauling my copy? Couldn't his subtext be interpreted as, "put out, baby, or your work will suffer?"

Hell!

How did I get into this professional/sexual *relationship*, anyhow?

There was only one person to blame . . . if Harry hadn't looked like my renowned Brit . . .

I pondered what this meant.
Was I suffering from PDS?

There is a psychological disorder called Personality Dependency Syndrome.

PDS is a neurosis where a person is only concerned with a famous actor or actress. It's said that many journalists suffer in the grip of this disease and spread it through their media coverage on television and in print. They convey that the normal, everyday life of the audience seems pointless when compared with the glam existence of a celebrity. Warnings have been issued by prominent psychologists that the ingredients of this disorder—sex, royalty, affluence, show business—are so important to the public that we may have a mental-health crisis!!

Oh, Gawd! What the hell was the answer?

Did I have PDS? Did all media suffer from this disorder? I simply didn't know.

What I did know was that Harry was on his way here to collect his pound of flesh . . . so to speak.

— 3 —

I HAD TO RUN, RUN, RUN. I slipped out of my door as quietly as I could so that Percy Kendricks, my neighbor, wouldn't hear me. This was quite hard, because I lived in a brownstone where all the stairs creaked. The real estate agent advised that this was good just in case robbers or rapists happened to stop by.

"Is that you, Lizzie?" Percy called as I rounded his landing.

"I'm in a hurry."

"If you're going to the gourmet shop, would you get me some duck confit?"

"Not going there."

"Where *are* you headed?"

His trained actor's voice resounded through the hall, though he still hadn't made an appearance—thespian Percy felt he had to be dressed properly to poke his head out the door. I could avoid him if I ran hard.

"Lizzie—wait." I heard his door slam when I reached the first-floor landing. Then, "Okay, I'll catch you on the way back."

I vaulted the three steps to the sidewalk and tossed the garbage in the proper receptacle, hoping Percy wouldn't be incensed enough to poke his head out the window and call out, "Shameless hussy!" the way he had one day when he was really mad at me.

I was lucky. He didn't.

I ran to the corner and slipped into the gourmet shop, quickly grabbed three bags of potato chips, three Perugina bars, two bottles of Pellegrino water, and two bagels. Paying quickly, I wondered whether I could sneak back home before Harry appeared.

I turned the corner and stopped cold. On the stoop, Harry Archer stood talking furiously with Percy. Percy was pointing in my direction, so I sneaked into a doorway, though I couldn't get much farther. These days every door in Gotham is locked.

I was contemplating my next move when a sweet-faced tourist handed me a five-dollar bill. "Here, dear. Take care of yourself."

She thought I was a homeless bag lady! Oh, my.

"No. It's okay," I said, handing her back the moxie.

She shrugged her shoulders. "False pride won't get you into heaven."

She walked away swiftly, sturdy heels banging on the concrete.

In her wake, my beloved appeared.

"Okay, Lizzie, what the hell are you doing lurking in that doorway—and why do you look like Little Orphan Annie in drag?"

— 4 —

Little Orphan Annie in drag?

Not me. I'm determined to be the most sturdy of the crazy

Parsons women. I'm a New York University graduate, *summa cum laude.* I have a career as a film critic, a 401K plan, an exquisite apartment, and a safety deposit box of jeweled memories. What more evidence that I'm a stalwart Gotham citizen?

I looked deeply into Harry's eyes for some indication that he cared for me. But all I saw was *rabid* L U S T!!! Upset by this, I dropped the chocolates. When I bent to retrieve them, he spotted my red bikinis.

Handsome Harry's voice got a little thick. "Just call me Daddy Warbucks. Let's go upstairs and shag."

"No dice," I said grimly.

Suddenly Harry looked melancholy, noticeably different from his normal devil-may-care persona. A far darker and slightly grumpy Harry emerged. His gloomy expression was that of a frustrated cad who'd unleashed his usually-successful-on-all-girls courtship and was furious to learn that I was an individual.

"Get off this attitude," he demanded, again acting as my official boss and not my bedmate.

Something in my head began buzzing, clanging, chinging—and then it all turned quiet and blank. "Your editing on my piece was an attack on women," I accused.

"I really like your piece," he responded with a salaciousness I found hard to accept under the circumstances.

Hell! Where was my serious, intelligent, charming Harry? Had he morphed into Daniel Cleaver (Bridget Jones' lover, an obsessive-compulsive Casanova who didn't care for the subtleties of Bridget's emotional needs, only focusing on her erotic ones? Which, I have to say, were quite hot.)

My path was clear. Caving to this man (however adorable he was) would go against the grain of Alice Parsons' grandkid. I wasn't going to be a slave to my desires, no matter how exciting, without so much as an "I'm sorry about that tart, Sherry, who was hanging on my arm last night and who I may have shagged . . . just to be polite!"

Nosirree!!

Here was a man who'd probably been the reason for more than one woman's hopeful fantasies turning bad, who'd spent his life up to now breaking women's hearts, who showed no inclination to change. And now that I was his current prey, he was ruthlessly exploiting my emotional vulnerability, pretending he had no baggage of his own, that I was the one who was encumbered.

Well, I had enough evidence to hang Harry, but it wasn't making me happy. Instead, I felt like Jane Austen schmaltz.

Harry smiled, putting his arms around me. When I pushed him away, he turned livid.

"Look, Lizzie. Stop all this prick-teasing nonsense. You're sending mixed signals. First you devour me, then you turn icy cold. I've a good mind to report you to your precious JANO crew. I'm sure this bitch titillation routine is against Jane Austen's proper rules."

Then he abruptly turned and walked into the sunset before I could stop him.

Oh, Gawd!

I began shaking badly. Harry had read ALL of Jane Austen and knew her preferences for truth and honor in the face of almost everything that could happen to a person. And he knew that I knew that he was right.

Ohmigod!

That makes two strikes against me.

In the JANO rulebook that meant I could be permanently exiled.

Chapter Seven

— 1 —

I RETURNED HOME TO BEGIN preparing my JANO defense, barely getting started before the phone rang.

"Wow," Fancy said. "What on earth did you do to the good old boy?"

"Nothing. That's the problem."

"Well, he said to tell you to bust your ass to get the copy for *The Fist* in early tomorrow."

"But I didn't see the film . . ."

"Yes, but Harry didn't notice."

"Harry didn't notice anything but Sherry."

"Don't go on about that. I hear she's been calling him every half-hour, and Sally tells me he doesn't take her calls."

Sally was *The Record*'s receptionist and on our side.

"Well, he came down here and demanded sex, but I told him to go shove it."

"Nicely, nicely, I hope."

"Not too nicely."

"Ah, come on, Lizzie. Remember we're Austen Girls. We do it with style."

"We try."

On the computer, I was scanning for theaters where *The Fist* was showing. Damn. It was a limited release; only at the Signet theater in Chelsea, not one of my fave places anytime—especially at night.

"Look, I can make the seven o'clock show, come home, write the review, and fax it to you. Okay?"

"Want to meet for a drink?"

"Too distracted. I have something really important to do."

"Gabriel?"

"Huh?" I'd forgotten about my treachery scenario.

"The Hunk. Remember?"

"Oh. Too much has happened too fast. I gotta go."

"Keep your skivvies on . . ." Fancy turned Brit when she wasn't getting enough attention.

I ran to my closet and grabbed a black-on-black outfit, black leather pants, jacket, T-shirt, silver jewelry, dark glasses. Hopefully no one would recognize me looking like an escapee from a biker flick.

When I got to the Signet, the usual crush of popcorn-munching people stood waiting on line. Because I benefitted from perks like screenings and videotapes, the prospect of walking into a movie theater with the public was scary. In the horrible event that I needed to do that, I'd usually choose noontime, when senior citizens attend. Then all I had to watch for was that the crowd didn't rustle too many bags. (Some of the aged crowd seem overloaded with shopping bags. I don't know why.)

As I waited, a man behind me bent my ear about the frustrations of trying to squeeze into these tiny theaters and the long lines for good films. When we finally gained admission, he kept carping about all the good seats being taken—we'd have to settle for miserable ones.

I ran away from him instantly, settling into an end seat in the back row. The way I figured it, I'd only have to watch thirty minutes of this testosterone epic to write a decent review.

Okay, I'll confess. The setup is everything to a critic—mostly because we never reveal how a film ends. Anything else I needed, I could swipe from the publicity packets I'd gotten at last night's screening.

But it wasn't to be. Ten minutes into the film, the sound went dead. Jeers mounted to ominous levels. Suddenly, it was zoo time in Gotham. People got up from their seats and shouted, "Yo! No sound!" to the projection booth. Obviously, no one was there, because nothing happened. Threats followed in various Latino dialects I didn't understand. Three kids marched up and down the center aisle in unison, clenched fists raised to the sky, imitating the costumed hero of the film.

The manager, a man with a reed-thin body and a slim pinkish nose, tried to calm the audience. Mass refusal. Arguments went back and forth until he promised to refund tickets with cold cash. But many patrons refused to budge. When I asked the manager where else the film was playing, he muttered, "Forty-second Street."

No way I was going up to that den of urban sin. So I watched the film without sound—probably a good thing, except for the fact that several in the audience kept shouting out their choices for dialogue. They were obviously fans of the comic book hero—though I don't think words like m . . . f . . . k . . . could possibly play such a big part in a youth-marketed book.

Pop!! A foil-wrapped candy hit the left lens of my glasses. It felt like a bullet. These days, this was not a paranoid thought. Quickly, I scrunched down, trying to come up with a plan. Should I crawl my way up to the entrance?

"Oh, sorry," someone said before I made my move. I turned to see Maxim Lester, once a regular on television. His specialty was playing the kind of person who, if you noticed him following you down a city street, you'd get the heebie-jeebies and yell for the cops.

Today Maxim looked pretty good, dressed in the sort of clothes I'd choose. Nice tight trousers, denim jacket, dark blue shirt, no jewelry, terrific trainers.

"Hellooooo, Ms. Eliz-a-beth!" he drawled in a bayou accent as he sat next to me. "How are you enjoying the flick? Did you see my walk-on?"

Of course I had. I was a film critic, damn it, not a floozie out for an hour and a half of mindless film watching. I nodded, turned away, and hoped he'd disappear.

"You knoooow . . ." he continued that odd drawl, "if you were to mention me in your review, I would be ever so, so marvelously, thankful." He batted his too-long eyelashes. I wondered if they were real.

"Oh, so you're off the stuff?" I said much too bluntly.

He nodded in a way that reminded me of Pip in *Great Expectations* after that awful girl turned him down. Suddenly I felt guilty over everything that happened to Maxim.

I brought myself up short. "How'd you do that?"

He smiled. "An actor's technique—how to manipulate the audience."

This was totally annoying. "You've got to get an audience first." I spit out the words as I mercilessly attacked him. "And since you're an alarmingly bad actor . . ."

Posthaste his tears appeared, so I bit my tongue to stop talking. How could I be so insensitive to this man who was in the toughest business in the world? He needed simple human kindness, and here I was being a prima donna film critic.

"Sorry. Sorry. Sorry," I apologized.

Oddly, his expression changed and he began sweating profusely. "Do you want me?" Maxim whispered.

Cripes! Was this every man's reaction to any sweet thing a

girl said? Yessirree. Men basically believe that everything a lady does or says has to do with sex. Hell, maybe they're right.

"Look, you're lovely, but I'm in the middle of a two-man jousting match—the last thing I need is a third backup."

"Don't be cynical, Elizabeth. It's wonderful when men fight over a girl. Think about all those girls who don't have anyone fighting over them." Maxim took a deep breath. "I'm essentially a good-natured guy. I'm funny and likable. I could help you out. How about a quickie?"

"Tempting—but no thanks. Maxim, dearest, be a good actor and leave me to do my work."

What bull. Yet, with an astonished look, the actor left, though he was growling like a bear. Intent on watching my reaction to the film, Maxim retreated into a seat across the aisle.

Oh, Gawd.

Whatever happened to the fun of going to films, when they were so good that afterwards I thought about them for days? I'd smile and talk like Julia Roberts, imitate her walk, dress in Julia clothes.

That's when I strolled the funky Village streets and dreamt of another kind of life.

I was *veree* happy—and I owed it all to films.

— 2 —

BACK HOME, I CHECKED my machine for a call from Harry saying he was sorry for everything. Instead, I heard Edgar's voice asking that I attend tomorrow's JANO meeting because something *veree* important had to be addressed.

YIPES!! Gabriel must have ratted me out.

I couldn't do much about it now, so I went to work. Damn! I wish I didn't have to concentrate on that awful film. But now that I was a film critic, I had to watch films with too critical an eye, had to know too much about what happened both on the set and behind the scenes. I had to be completely aware of things I hated like costs, profits, and deals.

I checked the publicity packet for *The Fist*. All the usual information was there, how this was a pioneering film with the most advanced technology . . . blah, blah, blah. . . pages of sleazy publicity stuff.

Okay. Let's review the bitch . . .

Is *The Fist* an empty exercise in camp, or is it a lovingly crafted exercise to regress audience members back to their forgotten childhoods when life was simpler and every boy believed in heroes and villains? Or is it simply an example of our ironically empty pop culture, a culture which has depleted all sense of quality on every level?

To say *The Fist* is cheap action material is to give it more than it deserves. The violence is in wild disproportion to the actual conflict of the story. Every difficulty is met with a slam-bam encounter. Each fight is a spar-box-punch-joust-slug-combat, executed in a gleeful stylistic hyperbole which leaves the audience cheering.

The film encourages everyone to admire violence. It puts us squarely into the territory of "brutality is the best response," without the exploration into serious male emotions like loyalty, passion, and grief.

If you like humiliation, overkill, and intentional crassness—see *The Fist*. Or you could save your money, turn on the television and watch a silly reality show.

I added in all the tchotchkes, cast, director, producer, etc., and faxed it to Fancy, who would see it in the early morning. When I fell asleep, I had nightmares about a huge fist silently pursuing me through the night. Funny thing, though, it quite resembled Harry's dick.

— 3 —

THE PHONE WOKE ME. "Lizzie, I love your review. It's savage. Absolutely brilliant."

Harry sounded drunk. I checked the clock. Five A.M. Workaholic Harry was at the office before the sun was up.

"Glad you like it," I managed to mumble.

"Now I really regret . . ." He choked on the words, so this was bound to be bad.

"Regret what?"

"Damn it, Lizzie. You made me so mad, I did something I shouldn't have."

"You shagged Sherry?"

"No, something important."

What could be more important than cheating on *moi*?

"I had drinks with Edgar. Forgive me, Lizzie. I had one too many."

"What did you say to him?"

"You don't want to know."

"Please . . . tell . . . me."

"Okay. But don't be mad?"

"Harry!!!"

"I told him you're a ball-busting bitch who wants it when you want it, and that you have no feelings about how a man who's in love with you might feel when you told him to fuck off."

"In love with me???"

"Yes." His voice cracked. "I'm in love with you. Only you're too busy with your damned Jane Austen guys to notice. Wake up, Lizzie. I'm a real, flesh-and-blood man who adores you. This is real life. This isn't a film."

– 4 –

My life is like a film.
The set is in my mind.

Almost always I can visualize the next scene in my life, then the one after that. I create the dialogue, prompt lines from the other actors, direct their expressions, make sure they know their marks on the set, and then we film the scene.

So, life goes on and on, scene by scene, each scene with a particular conflict I try to solve. I know if the conflict is not resolved, it will build to a crisis—and then I will be surely harmed.

That, in a nutshell, is my life's philosophy.
Only it doesn't always work.

Chapter Eight

— 1 —

HERE WE WERE, Maggie and Lizzie, mother and daughter, known to some as "hot" women, sitting on soft pale peach chairs and drinking martinis from tall blue glasses. The venue was Speakeasy, a Thirties-style hangout complete with faded green velvet curtains supposedly from Scarlett O'Hara's front parlor.

(I never really believed this, knowing how much money *Gone with the Wind* memorabilia went for.)

The place was funky yet serious, with ornate Art Deco furnishings plus a white grand piano in the corner. But Speakeasy wasn't as innocent as it pretended to be. When I ventured up the narrow stairs to the ladies' room, I saw pretty people dressed in black, smoking, popping pills, and who knows what else.

When I told my mother about them, she simply shrugged. "That's their life, not ours."

"Do you ever regret anything you've done?" I tried to look innocent as I began my entrapment regarding her nudie film.

She surprised me. "Sometimes I think everything I ever wrote should go up in flames. I feel terribly guilty, writing books that encouraged women to leave their husbands."

She paused. "I was at a panel just the other day. Some old bat came up to me and said, 'You know, Ms. Parsons, I read your book when I was forty. So I left my husband and have been lonely and desperate ever since.'"

Mom muttered, "That's what happens when you're an author. People crap all over you."

I laughed. "Have you seen my letter file?"

"All right, Lizzie. Always trying to do one better than your poor mum. Don't be selfish, darling. Let me have my crisis— let me enjoy it." She sipped her martini and added, "These days I'm thinking that everything we lived through in the Sixties and the Seventies was ONE BIG MISTAKE!!!"

"Does that include my birth?"

"No, darling. Of course not," Mom's startling blue eyes softened. "There is nothing in my life that I'm happier about than having you as my daughter. I'm so proud of you."

"Even more than your books?" I parried.

She smiled, her cheeks growing ever more vivid. She'd walked up to the Village from Tribeca, and the brisk Hudson River winds had heightened her already technicolor complexion.

"Even more," Mom whispered, giving me a quick kiss.

I continued my pursuit of the truth. "More than getting that super teaching job at the university?"

Her heavily made-up eyebrows arched. "Yes, even that."

"How about becoming infamous for your famous bod?"

I waited for her to turn purple and toss her too-long coif about, but Mom seemed perfectly at ease with my prying question. "What infamous event are you particularly referring to?" she asked while calmly playing with the lemon slice in her martini.

I didn't answer. Instead, I stared into the remnants in my glass, wondering why I'd downed the thing like there was no tomorrow.

With expert timing, Louis the bartender looked my way. Before my mother arrived, he'd been gleefully bad, offering a sarcastic commentary on life in the fast lane, punctuated with tales of women who had the most appalling fetishes. What Louis said gave me the willies—though his ice-blonde hair, clear grey eyes, and reddened lips (I do believe it was lipstick) atop a sinewy body encased in black leather wasn't bad to gaze at.

While Mom glared at me, waiting for an answer, Louis shook his head sympathetically and asked if I wanted more poison. I didn't want another martini so I ordered two, one with onion and one without.

Mom scheduled our martini get-togethers in memory of Gran, who'd lived a "martini life," a truly passé existence popular in the Thirties—which included being tipsy and witty every day of your life. Thankfully, this went out of fashion before I was born.

If the truth be known, Mom distrusted martinis after often finding her mother on the couch, passed out, clothed in various ensembles, a satin corselet being the most popular one.

Also, Mom was a Sixties survivor, an era when other forms of excess were popular.

Fortunately, women of my generation were cool about this kind of stuff, because we were into looking good. Every idiot girl sitting in Speakeasy looked fabulous. (I must remember never to take a man here.)

Most were flexible dressers, arriving in suits and Manolo Blahnik shoes. (How on earth did they walk around with those all day?) One-two-three, they'd shrug off their jackets and bam!—sheer blouses, sequined T-shirts, black lace bras made their appearances.

Although I was similarly dressed, it was Mom who could compete with the best of them. Her tight red leather skirt, low-cut satin top, spiked heels, and floppy hat passed the test. Because her best friend Adrienne (makeup artist to the stars) had convinced her that appearing in public sans full face was tantamount to treason against the female of the species, Mom wore full cosmetic regalia. The startling purple-blue eye makeup, the porcelain pancake (almost the bloom of English gals), and tinted cheekbones hinted that this fifty-plus gal had gone for a tasty face lift. (Not true.)

I admired Mom for keeping up appearances, but frankly I didn't really want to be a fifty-plus woman batting false eyelashes at every man in the room.

That is truly unattractive.

"You really are wearing much too much makeup," I said rather unpleasantly.

Swiftly, Mom changed the subject from blasting her to blasting me. "Lizzie, you are from a family of beautifully cosmetic women. Stop trying to change your genes. How about a little more eyeshadow, and . . ."

Totally annoyed, I said, "Don't be a bore!!"

"Darling, you don't get to sip your martini and judge me. It's a bad habit you have."

Still, I felt harsh. "Have you told me everything that happened to you in the Sixties?"

With that, Mom looked guilty. Her jaw literally dropped. "You don't really know what happened when your father and I fell in love, do you?"

She didn't wait for an answer. "Daddy came across as a dreamy poet, and I was his rock, the realist who paid the bills. We were intensely in love and didn't care if we had nothing to eat or drink. What was money compared to what we had with each other?"

She popped an onion from my martini into her mouth, munched on it leisurely, then swallowed it too quickly, which caused her eyes to pop like Ally McBeal's always did. "I would do anything Daddy wanted me to do."

Her eyes crossed slightly as she added, "Sam told me he phoned you about the nudie. It was your father's idea, darling. I simply couldn't refuse him."

Was she telling the truth? "But you left him!"

"I did just that. Finally. But that's because he cheated on me." Her eyes grew teary now. "I mean, he cheated on us."

She reached for my hand and held it tightly as moisture from her eyes etched two trails through the thick makeup. Exasperated, she took out a makeup case and repaired the damage. After smothering her lips with tons of gloss, she continued speaking in a neutral voice, as if talking about someone else. I'd seen her like this before. It always worried me.

"I finally was on my own," she said solemnly. "That's when everything got hard. You didn't know what I went through. I had to take care of you. I didn't know how to earn a good living." She choked on the next words. "I didn't know who I was going to meet, and if I was going to meet anyone. I didn't know where we were going to wind up."

Between each of these confidences, she sighed deeply. Quite a performance, I thought. "If I remember correctly, you had plenty of opportunities," I said bitchily.

She bitched back. "Don't be smug—it's not polite in a saloon."

But I kept on track. "Sam said the film is being shown at the Spring Festival. These days, you're a respected intellectual. What are they going to say at the university when someone prints the fact that Maggie Parsons was once a nudie star?"

My mother laughed. "Don't be so naive, Lizzie. That was a long time ago, and besides, everybody in the university hierarchy lived through the Sixties . . . in those days we were much more sexually repressed than kids are now, but we were real romantics."

"Puh-leeze . . ." I protested.

She eyed me cruelly. "Yes, I know it didn't work for me and tons of other women. But your generation doesn't believe in love at all. You're all going to end up without any memories."

"Hey, maybe that's okay."

Her arm shot up to make the sign of the cross, something Mom did whenever she needed a powerful exclamation point. I waited with baited breath for her next pronouncement.

"Don't you know, darling, that a life without ghosts is not a life worth living?"

$$- 2 -$$

Maggie's ghosts.

My mother grew up backstage in dressing rooms before Social Services scooped children away from their moms. In fact, when I saw *Chicago,* I wept. Roxie Hart could have been dear Gran.

Alice Parsons was peroxide blond until her dying day. She was *tres* tiny and drank an extra dry martini with two olives at lunch, often wearing a black corselet with tiny pink ribbons at each naughty place.

Alice never disclosed who my grandad was. She described him only as a "classy gent but a bit of a daddy's boy." I liked that phrase, and as a girl was fond of calling most men "daddy's boys"—which puzzled quite a few.

During their affair, Daddy's Boy offered Gran a beautiful Park Avenue apartment, a generous allowance, and told her she didn't have to work anymore. She said "no thanks." Later she married him but kept hoofing until she was in her forties. That's when Daddy's Boy was killed in the War and she found herself with an inheritance.

After that, Gran lived out her life serving lunch and playing pinochle to an assortment of odd types. My favorites were Mom's godparents: Uncle Guys, a cigar-toting Wall Street stock broker who was "queer," and Eddie Synge, who was distantly related to the great Irish playwright and read erotic poetry to anyone who would listen.

Yet, for all of this eccentricity, Mom's schooling was really conservative. Gran sent her to Sacred Heart Academy, where the children of Manhattan's rich Irish called shagging "fornication" and believed it was Satan's way of kidnaping our souls to hell.

Mom laughed them off, but something must have stuck. When she was a hippie and got pregnant, she and Dad choose not to have an abortion the way any drug-taking-wine-soaked-counter-culture types would have. Instead, Mom went home, and I was ushered into the world at St. Vincent's Hospital in the Village—a few blocks from where I live now.

This is my inheritance . . . along with a safe-deposit box full of diamond chokers, bracelets, rings, and pins—all from Grandmother Alice.

– 3 –

THROUGHOUT MY CHILDHOOD, I was constantly lectured. My mother's way to counteract the Propaganda of Womanhood, POW for short, was to incorporate absolute reality into everyday living.

(One of her views was that family survival depended on the woman in the kitchen. I know this is old-fashioned, but my rebellious Mom is a great gourmet cook.)

Romance was not a staple in our lives. Not ever. But devotion was. Mom was devoted to all sorts of things. Her Betsy Johnson silver mini, circa 1966. Tons of geometric plastic jewelry. Two Beatles T-shirts signed by John and Paul, respectively. A Mary Quant makeup bag. And a treasured copy of Julie Christie in *Darling*.

In addition to these superficial things, Mom also weighed in on the spirit of the Sixties. "Always be true to your friends, never leave them for a guy, don't have babies unless you can support them alone, and remember sex is truly special—so don't waste it on creeps."

I learned to admire her. Not a complaining type, Mom devoted her life to "living in the now." She tried her hand at designing clothes, did a stint as a shoe model, bartended, and searched for a way to nurture our lives.

But my mother's real gift was living by instinct. She stopped using drugs before becoming addicted, stopped shagging about before AIDS, and had a perpetual sense of how to survive the madness of the world she preferred.

As a result, she was the only survivor of her group who'd come of age in that strange, exciting era: the Sixties.

"I must go on without them," she'd say when we looked at the photographs and souvenirs of that time.

That's when I knew she was lonely.

– 4 –

MOM ALWAYS HAD A WAY out of sadness. When I complained about having an absent dad, she invented the phone call. I don't know where she got the continually changing numbers, but she'd give me one, take me to a public phone booth, and wait while I dialed. Then she'd tell me to ignore the noise at the other end of the line, and simply say what was in my heart.

I'd say, "Hello, Dad. How are you? Mom and I are doing okay. I got an A in English. I want to be a writer. I love film stars. How are you?"

Mom would stand there and listen and not interfere until I got to the important question, "Daddy? Why did you leave us?"

That's when she'd depress the lever, and the phone call was over.

Afterwards, we'd go to a film. Mom's therapy was to explain that life was like a film, and that because too many disasters spoiled a film, I must be cool in life.

I learned my lessons well. I'm sure that's why I'm a film critic and not a screenwriter. You see, criticism allows me to tear apart any notion that there is such a thing as a "perfect" film (or a "perfect" life).

And whenever I'm really down, a public phone and random dialing works for me.

Chapter Nine

— 1 —

I WALKED ALONG PARK AVENUE SOUTH, headed for the Gramercy Park Hotel and the JANO meeting while I thought about Mom, me, and the rest of the girl world.

(Does everyone have this kind of mental dialogue? I especially suffer from discourses like these when I'm doing silly things like picking up groceries or heading someplace where I expect disaster.)

I felt a damp hand on my arm and abruptly switched to Gotham paranoia mode—a quirky survival instinct which, if one is not a Manhattan resident, should be treated with tranqs. Sure enough, a homeless man was caressing my arm from the gutter. No suitor he—his beard was filthy, his stinking clothes disheveled, and he was sans shoes—dirty sewer water covered his feet with black goop.

I tried to slip from his grasp, but his arms flailed in a counter-clockwise motion, his long, ragged nails flickering in the sunlight like the gnomon on a sundial. Unfortunately, he took a long step towards me and when close, opened his mouth. His breath was foul, with few teeth in evidence.

"Are you hungry?" I asked, too meekly.

He laughed and hopped about on one foot with glee. "Yes! Yes!"

I dug into my purse for cash. "Buy yourself a sandwich." I handed him the loot, but he shook his head. The currency fell to the grimy curb.

"Well, what do you want?" I asked, getting angry, though I tried to keep in mind that this person was homeless and therefore deserved my complete compassion. Considering the fact that I was about to be roasted by my fellow JANO-ites, I didn't have much compassion on hand.

I looked into the man's bloodshot eyes and saw his frenzy. Frightened, I took a step backwards, but he lurched forward to paw at my hand. I'm sorry to report that I pushed him away.

In a hoarse voice he shouted, "You got an extra bottle of Viagra?"

Whot????

Several passersby stared but, coward that I am, I fled down the street. At the corner, I turned to watch from a safe distance. Like a gonzo wizard from *The Lord of the Rings,* he chanted whilst stomping up and down in the dirty sewer water. *"You got an extra bottle of Viagra? Do ya? Do ya?"*

Several onlookers laughed. One guy scribbled down the words, probably planning to use them in his next album . . . which would probably go gold. People would sing "You got an extra bottle of Viagra? Doo-wop! Doo-wop!"

The image delighted me. But one short, squat passerby was not amused. "You're too damned old for Viagra," he shouted, his voice cruel.

The homeless man went deaf and dumb, looking terribly sad. I was overcome by compassion and forced myself to retrace my steps and offer him comfort. "Don't worry," I said, overdoing the nice bit. "What you need is a simple cleanup. Why don't you go to the YMCA? Get a shower or something. Here, take this."

Stupidly, I handed him my YWCA card. It was for the women's branch, but they'd make an exception in this case—wouldn't they?

"*Everybody needs love,*" he whispered.

$$- \: 2 \: -$$

THERE WAS NO LOVE at the JANO meeting. If ever there was a negative Jane Austen experience . . . this was it.

The meeting was a sort of courtroom lineup. Edgar sat in the center of a long table, arms crossed, wearing an off-duty outfit, a purple silk Nehru jacket which he hoped transformed him to a James Ivory lookalike.

Edgar was deeply impressed by the director of E.M. Forster's films, *A Room with a View* and *Maurice.*

Unfortunately, the jacket did not transform Edgar into the elegant Ivory. He looked more like an aged chorus dancer who'd forgotten the steps.

"We've had several serious complaints about you," Edgar said, pointing his index finger at me.

I noticed his cheeks were very puffed up and wondered whether he'd been crying. To get into character, so to speak, my eyes moistened as I bent my head in real, personal pain.

(At least I hoped that was what I was conveying.)

"Edgar, dear, you've known me for a *veree* long time and have observed my behavior in the most dire of circumstances," I said as sweetly as I dared.

"Yes, Lizzie dear. You haven't had an easy time. But still . . . we have our JANO rules and regulations, don't we?"

Gabe snickered. "Ha! It's about time."

I took a deep breath and assessed the climate. It was early, and there were only three JANO-ites present. Gabe was wearing one of his precious torn T-shirts along with tight, tight cutoff jeans.

Uh-oh—I'd better not think of the state of my love life, or Fancy's serious advice. If I did that, Gabe would be back in the running. That would make matters much worse.

I concentrated on Jane Austen's Rules of Hostility as exemplified in that remarkable book about gossip, manipulation, busybodying, and the like: *Emma.*

Emma is vain, self-centered, careless of the feelings of others. And she's mean!

Remember her treatment of poor Miss Bates at the Box Hill picnic?

Yes, Emma's behavior reflected the civilized Jane Austen way to act out hostility:

1. Always be polite.
2. Say "Please, Madam" (if a gal), "Sir" (if a guy) before you say anything hostile.
3. Always use wit and charm to convey "Fuck you."
4. Afterwards, say "Thank you for your time."
5. And SMILE!

— 3 —

"LOOK, DARLINGS. . . ." I drawled the last word, trying to sound as much like Lady Catherine de Bourgh as possible. (Remember her in *Pride and Prejudice?* She was the old bat with all the money!)

I tried the breathless non-stop approach made popular in those French New Wave films of the Sixties. "This first date bit is never a clean hit for me. When I dated Gabe, I felt his history with exes and present ladies was there with us as I was slugging back wine and analyzing how my thighs looked in the dress I spent much too much money for."

Gasping quickly for air, I continued. "Well—Gabe sweet-talked me into his bed—which I might add, he did in no time at all! But afterwards there were all sorts of rules—stuff like I can't ask him anything at all about other girls. If I asked him any questions, he came down with the most peculiar speech impediments."

(Where was I going with this? I simply didn't know.)

Gabe flew off the handle. "It's all a lie!"

"You're a terrible snob, Lizzie," Babs said as she joined the jury of my peers. Today, Babs was wearing a rock ensemble: hot pants accessorized with a tight bra and a belt with spiked studs.

That was definitely the snobbiest trick! How dare she call me a snob? This East Coast WASP's attempt at street chic was absurd. If you're a proper blue-blooded eccentric, act like it, for heaven's sake. Stop trying to emulate poor working girls whose talents and perseverance earned them everything the world had to offer: men, money, and fame.

Besides, Babs' imitation only resulted in downgrading her own charisma. Snobbery of that kind is a self-defeating weapon—it's always the snob who ends up looking cheap, not the people she's imitating.

"Hey, like your duds," Gabe said to her, wanting to annoy me. "Who's it all for?"

Babs' lips pursed. "I'm seeing Dennis Matrix, the film producer."

"More like shagging him," I muttered, a bit unpleasantly.

Babs gave me a strange, sidewise look. "Have you done him too, Lizzie?" she asked with a savagery that was most unattractive for one of Jane's disciples.

I knew Matrix, all right. He'd married a friend of Fancy's,

Dottie Sutton, when she was still in high school. Matrix told her he wouldn't wed unless she went to a shrink. Their marriage lasted ten years, during which they consulted respective analysts twice a week and really had no need to speak to each other. After so much time shagging and not speaking, they divorced. That's when Matrix moved his analyst in—I guess we can assume they talked a lot.

After a cruel divorce, Dottie became an exotic dancer and recently a member of our JANO group, voted in last month while Babs was in Aruba. Because Dottie used her maiden name, Babs hadn't made the connection yet.

"Uh-oh," I murmured.

Edgar caught my drift. "Yes, well, Babs, settle yourself down here and let's keep our focus on Lizzie, shall we?"

He shrugged his shoulders as he looked at me with an inquiring expression. Was he wondering, as I was, whether Babs knew what the former Dottie Matrix looked like? Because she was expected at this meeting *veree* soon.

This was worrisome. I never thought I'd feel sorry for an exotic dancer, but if, in her usual self-effacing style, Babs started babbling tales of Dennis Matrix's bedroom antics, this might turn grim.

Besides, where the hell was the analyst wife he'd banished Dottie for?

— 4 —

I MOTIONED TO EDGAR that I needed a private moment. When we went into Gabe's dressing room, I spotted several leopard-print bras with matching thongs. "You see, he's not so very faithful either," I sputtered.

"You're going to have to defend yourself at the meeting, Lizzie. And remember, I can't be partial."

What the hell was this? I've listened to and adored Edgar for years, and now he's telling me that I had no status in his heart.

Edgar was a special male, wasn't he? Though he didn't illuminate us regarding his sexual preferences, I'd always assumed he was a *bit* gay. (What this meant, I simply didn't know.) And gay men are generally quite understanding of a girl's annoyance with men of the heterosexual persuasion.

So what shit was this? Was I to assume even though a man's sexual preference matched mine—i.e. he liked guys— his genes would never permit him to be a *mensch*?

Okay. I tried to be perfectly calm and *tres* professional. "Look, can you help me out of this mess?"

"Lizzie, dear, why am I here? Certainly not to spy on Gabriel's private lingerie collection." Edgar bent his head in a strange Buddha-like manner. "Besides, this may not mean that Gabriel is seeing other ladies."

Oh, no! Was Edgar telling me that Gabe liked to play dress-up with Victoria's Secret? If yes, how did he know this?

Hmmm. (I didn't like that much.)

"Edgar, darling, I asked to speak to you because you know what's going to happen when and if Dottie Sutton arrives and Babs discovers that she's Matrix's ex."

His eyes shone brightly. "It'll be an invigorating meeting, then."

Was Edgar anticipating a catfight?

"Invigoratingly bloody," I commented.

He nodded eagerly. "Listen, when I was an actor, I remember what my first director told me. The two leading ladies were scratching their eyes out just before my cue. One was throwing dishes right where my entrance was. So I said to the director, 'If I walk out there, I'm going to get smashed by flying china.'

"And he told me, 'Use that.' I asked, 'What on earth do you mean . . . I'm supposed to get a concussion?'

"And he said, 'You're in a comedy, goddamn it. Throw the china back at her.'"

With that, Edgar grinned and left the dressing room. I sat there a moment and opened a couple of drawers where there were boxer shorts, Bermuda shorts, and more bras. Hell! In the privacy of his dressing room, was Gabe some sort of transsexual, or were these bras simply on hand for potential sexmates?

Hey, he never offered me a bra. But to be fair, I really didn't wear one when he was around.

I washed my face with cold water and went out to rejoin the fray. In my absence Dottie Sutton had arrived.

— 5 —

OH, BOY! She'd arrived all right.

I don't know what she was trying achieve, but Dottie was wearing a slip dress which revealed the outline of her bountiful nipples and the edges of her bikini panties. However, she did not look really naked because on her ankles, wrists, fingers, and ear lobes were diamonds of various sizes and shapes.

Manolo Blahnik shoes completed her outfit, which meant she'd watched *Sex and the City.* Her black, spiky hair and her impish, dimpled face gave Dottie the look of a club kid about to perform some sort of madcap act.

As she took a seat next to Babs (ohmigod!) she popped a couple of pills into her mouth.

"Anyone want a Percocet—Ambien? Or maybeeeeee— since everyone here looks grossly upset—a Paxil?"

When no one took her up on her offer, she repackaged her stash and tried to settle into today's meeting. "What's it about?" she inquired.

"Lizzie is up for conduct unbecoming a Jane Austen lady," Babs replied.

"Jeez, what a bitch!" Dottie said compassionately, looking at me through her very thickly-mascara-ed lashes. Then she whispered to me, "Whatever you did, you should've used a different name. Whenever I want to be bitchy, I go to a new club and pretend my name is Gwendolyn. That way, I never get blamed for anything I do. After all, the whole point of sex is to act out, isn't it??"

She had a point.

Just then Rick Swenson, our ex-priest, walked in.

Rick's brown hair sported blond highlights which went perfectly with his black leather jacket and scruffy jeans—the ones with ragged holes in each knee. He had an obligatory matchstick in his mouth, working it between his teeth as he walked over to the refreshment table and poured a cup of coffee too quickly, spilling it right on his exposed knees.

"Oh, hell!" he swore.

"Are you inebriated?" Edgar blared. Looking a bit drunk himself, Edgar shook his head in exasperation.

We'd been through this before. When Rick first joined JANO, he'd drink before meeting times. But he realized that led him to say things he really didn't want to say. So now he drank coffee and preached even more than he ever had when he wore a Roman collar.

"Don't fret," Dottie said kindly as she reached for Rick's hand. "Lizzie's on the hot seat tonight."

He snatched his hand back as if it had been electrocuted.

I believe the reason for his precipitate response was that as she leaned forward, Dottie's boobs became quite visible.

Rick turned to his other side and Babs, then began preaching. "You people bring up all sorts of stuff that you have no right to. Things I wouldn't even ask my best friend, never mind a stranger. I don't think that's what Jane Austen had in mind."

"Remember Emma," Edgar said with great clarity.

"What about her?" Rick asked.

"Emma was always gossiping about everyone and sticking her nose into their business," Babs filled in.

"And does that give us the right to poke our heads into Lizzie's life?" Rick queried.

I could have kissed him right then and there. But Gabe stepped up to the plate. "Normally, maybe not. But it involves a fellow JANO-ite. Me!!!"

"Oh, I see," Rick said, obviously responding to how attractive Gabe was—which was easy to do.

"You know," Dottie said to Edgar, "You look just like that guy who directs all those films."

"Which guy?" I shot back.

"The director—what's his name? You know, *A Room with a View, Howard's End* and especially, *Maurice.* Yessirree. That film changed my life."

"How so?" Babs asked suspiciously.

"Well, Babsie . . ."

That's the moment I knew that Dottie must be aware about Babs and her ex-husband's communal cuddling.

— 6 —

OH, DEAR.

But Dottie kept on chatting, seemingly imperturbable. "You see, I used to notice men's eyes and hair and faces—

and not much else. But ever since I saw *Maurice,* I've become sexually liberated."

"How so?" Rick asked, interested.

Dottie smiled. "I walk along the street and notice butts. I never know whether they belong to a man or a woman until I look up." She took a deep breath and announced, "I've become a kind of buttock-y bisexual."

Then she batted her lashes and said, quite explicitly to Babs, "Let me introduce myself. My name is Dottie Sutton Matrix."

Babs croaked, "Oh, you're a lesbian?"

Dottie shook her head. "Sorry. No."

"How do you know that?" Babs kept up a desperate counter-terrorist interrogation.

You see, if Dottie were a lesbian, then Babs could forgive Matrix for shoving his ex-wife out the door in the early A.M. with just her nightie and absolutely no makeup.

Dottie was right on the mark. "Because I never get turned on by breasts. It's muscular shoulders and flat chests for me. Also, vaginas leave me cold. The real test is when I think of sex, I think of nice, large penises. In fact, big, inflated ones really do me up fine."

She paused. "That's one thing I really have to hand to my ex-husband. He had a really big one. But he mostly liked using it for his own purposes. Didn't like to share, if you know what I mean, Babsie."

I thought Babs was about to fall over. But I must admit, I was really happy. No one was interested in the charges against me anymore.

Edgar crossed his legs and held his right knee tightly as that leg involuntarily swung up and down like a saw. He was really enjoying this. Rick leaned back on his chair with a silly smile on his face. And Gabe's body was at complete attention—by which I mean every part of his body was hard.

Just what is it about a catfight that's so erotic to men? I dunno. As for myself, I rose and walked to the refreshment table to get out of the ring before the bell rang.

But dammit, Gabe moved too fast. He rose and grabbed Babs, put his arms around her, and whispered in her ear. He must have been telling her the most wonderful things, because suddenly all the puffiness in her face seemed to pucker out.

Then Gabe changed his body position so that she was getting his hard point, if you know what I mean.

She smiled and said, "Edgar, I really think we should address this thing with Lizzie."

Edgar became the high court judge again. "Yes, you're right. There have been two complaints about Lizzie's conduct."

"Two . . . ?" Gabe sputtered.

"Yes, the other one is confidential, so I can't reveal the person."

"She was fucking someone else. I knew it!!" Gabe dropped his affectionate hold on Babs and clicked his heels as if he was reporting for duty.

Edgar stood firm. "I don't think we have to discuss this further. I'll simply make a condition that Lizzie's conduct has to change."

He turned to me. "Lizzie, you've got to be kinder to the men in your life—and to men in general. You know we're not the enemy."

"But . . ." I couldn't defend myself, because then I'd have to admit that I was shagging Harry.

"Give her some penance, for God's sake, and let's get this over with," Rick screamed.

"Penance!" Dottie made a face. "That's an ugly, ugly word."

"Just simply try to be more like a gentlewoman," Babs said facetiously.

Yeah, like she was one.

"Jane Austen's women were never gentle. They had balls," I retorted. "And we're diluting them down to stupid, silly, simpering ladies. That's just not true."

"Nevertheless, Lizzie. There is something called civility. And we must—*must*—adhere to it. So simply keep that in mind when you're in a coupling."

(Edgar liked to call sex coupling.)

"Be more civil to men!" he admonished.

I felt my eyes moisten with bitter tears. Here was my mentor, whom I loved with my whole heart and soul, acting like every other man in my life. He was condemning me, telling me to do something that was against my nature.

I checked out the room. Babs looked satisfied that I had been chastised. Gabe and Ricky had that wild-eyed male look in their eyes, the kind men get before they shag you.

Only Dottie showed compassion. She put her finger up to her lips like Mom used to, mouthing the words, "keep quiet— we'll deal with this later."

Hmmm. My kind of girl.

Edgar turned officious. After someone's behavior was in question and sentence given, he always gave a lecture.

Smiling at the group, he said, "Now let's talk about Love in Jane Austen's day."

No one seemed interested, but he continued. "Jane knew that women had no right to a perfect love. Yet she wrote her books so that somehow—through her wonderful plots—they found their soul mates."

He looked at me. "Today, everything is too easy. There's a misconception that marriage doesn't work . . . it's more fun just to have sex and then go to the next party."

"Yessirree," Dottie said cheerfully.

"Well, it simply won't wash, Dottie."

"And what are we supposed to do when our loving husbands throw us out on the street?" she queried.

"Get thee to a nunnery," Rick squeaked.

Gabe laughed. "Oh, yeah."

Edgar gave them his Perry Mason stare. "Remember, Dottie. Some men are scoundrels—but not all men are."

She fought back. "Well, the next time you live your life as a woman let's see if you really believe that."

Edgar looked petulant. "Oh, now you're going to use the 'You don't know how it is to be a woman because you're a man' thesis." He sighed. "Truly bad for the human race."

Oh, yeah.

But he wouldn't let it go. "You know my theory about that. If we're all going to survive this horrid new century, we must work very hard to understand and be empathetic to each other. Even to scoundrels."

More political correctness bullshit!

Dottie must have read my mind. She stood up and announced regally, "Well, Edgar, I've something to say."

"Well, say it," our leader commanded.

"Good girls don't get the good guys. Only naughty girls do." Then she added, "Remember that, Lizzie!!!"

Then Dottie Sutton Matrix stomped out of the meeting.

Chapter Ten

— 1 —

THE FLOWER HOTEL IS ONE of my fave places, due to the fact that the lobby looks like the reception room on the Titanic (as seen in that blockbuster film), projecting me to that elegant time. Because the ceilings are mirrored, several versions of myself and other persons attending the Zachary-Storrs wedding in the Hyacinth Room were reflected upside-down.

Never in my wildest dreams did I think Bitsy Zachary would be a bride. At college she was an intense narcissist who assumed that all world events had her as a center.

After graduating, Bitsy became a hybrid—a conservative, politically progressive woman who often wrote those *cute* columns for various magazines—the ones about how girls could make it in the world.

After reading them I'd become *veree* depressed. According to Bitsy's reasoning, to create a healthy balance of marriage, career, and motherhood, women needed nannies, an incredibly understanding husband, and plenty of money.

I hate to say this, but Bitsy is an ugly woman. Her nose is beaky, her body taut (no softness visible anywhere), and at six foot three, she looks down at males and females alike. She's also brittle, sarcastic, and makes enemies wherever she goes. Naively, I assumed this meant she'd never marry.

Lo and behold, two months ago the ice queen melted. Excitedly, Bitsy phoned to boast, "Yes, Lizzie. I've got a man."

"Who's that?" I was quite shocked.

"Ernest Storrs."

She waited for a reaction, but I kept silent. "Yes, I know. It's true that Ernest has been married three times, thus three divorces on his record, though he's really not that kind of Manhattan flirt. He's truly sensitive and loving. I know, because he sends me roses every morning."

"Sounds lovely." I tried to modulate my jealousy. (Remember, I hadn't met either Harry or Gabe yet.)

"And most importantly, he's part of my tribe."

"Your tribe?"

"Oh. Don't know whether to blab about this." Several deep breaths later, she added, "uh, it's okay, I guess. You only write film reviews."

Happy with this insult, she rambled on. "Let's face it. We old-line WASPs don't talk about it much, but we have our tribes. Usually they don't mix well—mostly because they own different banks. But here in the City, we do tolerate each other, although we are also suspicious. That's why it's been so hard for me to get a hubby."

Boy, was I wrong! I thought it was because Bitsy was nasty and ugly.

She gurgled on. "Ernest is a chieftain in our tribe. He owns Storrs Investments, our brokerage house, and is from old money."

I always had the suspicion that old money was kept in storage tins hidden beneath Park Avenue's lower levels.

"Where did you find your prince?"

"Lizzie, you don't have to be so blunt." (What was she talking about?) "I know that Ernest has a reputation as a womanizer," she cooed. "But we have to accept our men as they are. We can't change them."

Why was she telling me this? Did she know about my failed attempts at relationships?

Besides, how did Bitsy No-man get so wise in the how-to-get-along-with-a-man stuff? Did the knowledge come with the engagement ring?

"So expect a wedding invitation soon," Bitsy told me.

I remember signing off and thinking, *yeah, right*. But a wedding invitation *did* arrive. That's why Fancy (I was allowed an escort) and I were at the Flower Hotel.

In the elevator a slim, blow-dried straight-haired type dressed in pastels said to her friend, "Have you slept with Ernest, too?"

When the friend said "yes," it delighted Fancy so much that she tapped me hard. Since my skirt was tight, one of the side seams split.

"Good thing I have safety pins," my practical buddy whispered. No wonder. Fancy's outfits had been getting increasingly diaphanous. She wore a sarong silk wrap accessorized with a rhinestone brooch holding her tiny bra top in place.

Thank heavens we decided to skip the serious part of the wedding celebration. Would St. Thomas Episcopal Church have allowed us into their hallowed halls?

But this was party time at the Flower Hotel (where many scandals had occurred, so the gossip columns say).

— 2 —

AS WE WALKED INTO the Hyacinth Room, I realized that even wealthy people have to exert themselves for romance. The bar was in full swing as the ten-piece orchestra played crappy tunes. Lots of networking was going on. Groups greeting other groups, men and women shaking hands as they conducted themselves according to Park Avenue society rules.

Everyone looked married. Confident, stout women led red-cheeked escorts to tables displaying breathtaking floral centerpieces and exquisite china settings. As they checked table placements, they turned increasingly frantic. (In this society, where one sat was extremely important).

The oval-shaped room also sported one long table surrounded by constantly swirling rows of candles for the wedding party. Fancy and I searched for our table and found five women seated there. All, I'd wager, were unmarried.

"Oh, fuck!" Fancy exclaimed. "The spinster table."

Our dinner companions looked scandalized and continued their conversation in the low, earnest voices one expected from wealthy New Yorkers. They all looked hungry, and when the hors d'oeuvres were served, scooped them up, leaving none for us.

What a blank bunch! They looked the same—too-long, straw-blond hair, receding chins, pouty lips (treated ones, I'll bet), and singularly goose-like necks sporting the family's real pearls. Oh, and they wore expensive black halter dresses and the pointy toed sandals which were featured on every fashion magazine cover this month.

I decided to be polite. "Hi, I'm Elizabeth Parsons."

The girls stared at me as if to deny my existence. I slunk

down further in my seat, trying to consider how to screw these tarts.

Though I was not as adventurous as Fancy, neither in remarks nor in dress, I was wearing a see-through black sheer blouse (like the one Bridget wore which got Daniel Cleaver's attention), tight satin skirt (also, like Bridget's), and spike satin pumps on my feet, complemented by black lace mesh stockings.

"Not bad," Fancy whispered as she noted our companions' more conservative—i.e., *boring*—mode of dress.

"Not bad yourself!" I remarked.

Aside from her diaphanous outfit, Fancy's tawny-colored legs were naked, and she'd painted sequined hearts on her toe-nails, matching the ones on her eloquent fingernails.

Swiftly, my galpal signaled the waiter, and soon those fingers were entwined around a tall, pink glass which contained a very stiff martini. Since our table was quite close to the serving bar, Fancy turned her chair so that her crossed legs, swirling to and fro, were aimed to catch the attention of any male who happened by.

The men came in all sizes and shapes, bringing joy and hope to my dear friend. No fashion faux pas could ever rival the speedy way they stopped at her chair, introduced themselves while enjoying her burgeoning bosom (quite noticeable, due to that expensive sequined skin toner she'd used.) All acted in the most insinuating manner of a CIA agent and that kind of awful person.

The oddest thing was that none of them asked Fancy to dance. I wondered about that and first was very unhappy at the thought that they were racist. But that didn't seem likely— these folks were hypocrites and would never reveal that kind of behavior in public.

Finally the answer hit me. They were all *with* someone— unlike everyone at our outcast table. So they could flirt, perhaps drop off cards, talk to us . . . but didn't want to get caught actually dancing with one of the *spinsters*, however sexy we might be.

Oh, Gawd! Why did I decide to come to this wedding? I was already tired of the pastel-colored room with its devotion to seventeenth-century French furniture, the soft tones of the orchestra still living in the Forties, and the clusters of blossoms bursting forth on every table. I began tapping my feet on the marble floor and was rewarded with astonished looks from the debutantes.

I was forming a *veree* hostile reply when the wedding party arrived. Bitsy was covered in eggshell-colored satin up to her neck. Her long wedding train was antique lace with pearls. She looked horrible. The groom was *veree* short and only reached Bitsy's flat chest. He had a round face and pudgy lips, reminding me of all those spoiled French counts who got sex because they had cash.

The happy couple sat in regal chairs, with best man and ladies in waiting on either side. When the toasts began I zombied out—a wonderful technique I'd learned in high school whenever I was bored with a subject.

"You all right?" Fancy asked, looking a bit concerned.

"Are my eyes crossed?"

"Sure are."

"I don't know why we came," I growled.

"You wanted hard evidence—if Bitsy gets married, anybody can wed."

I was troubled. "I don't understand what's happening to me. You know our rule, the only thing you need to get a man is ANOTHER MAN?"

Fancy nodded. "You betcha!"

"It's not working for me," I complained.

"Look, Lizzie. You've got two terrific men hot for you, but you're not satisfied, are you?"

"No, I'm not."

"That's because you're terribly fussy. You wouldn't marry an Ernest Storrs, would you?"

"God, no!" I said with much vehemence.

Across the table, the five played with their pearls the way society girls do to express their indignation. I swear I heard them whisper, "tsk-tsk."

Hey—where did they come from? Weren't we the NEW Girls—the *Sex and the City* babes?

Apparently not.

— 3 —

I BEGAN TO CALM DOWN as the champagne was poured. Silently I indulged in the truffled duck liver pate, the salad of yellow beets in fig syrup, the succulent duck with saffron rice and green-pea puree, and the endless variety of berry tarts accompanying cups of coffee which hopefully would sober us up.

But Fancy wasn't having any. My girlfriend had insisted on drinking more than her share of martinis, reminding me of Gran.

I leaned over to my dearest friend and whispered, "My Gran drank martinis. She said they were sexy."

Fancy went right to it. "Yes, but that was a time when women had to make up excuses for wanting sex. We don't have to do that. Our problem is to get these idiot guys to cooperate and not give us a lot of grief. Imagine, for years and years, men have said they wanted girls who wouldn't hold them up for marriage and mortgages. And now that we are in a position due to the scientific gains of the last fifty years—

you know, birth control devices and other stimulants of brain activity that produce immediate sexual hunger—"

She gasped for a breath. "We are the women men have ALWAYS WANTED. . . . so why do they still give us a HARD TIME?"

Boy, she was drunk. "Guess that makes them hard," I teased.

She sent me a woeful glance. "Just do not be funny about this *veree* serious matter. The future of the human race is at stake, Lizzie. For if we don't cohabit—the race dies out."

"Hey, I'm tired of coping with relationships. Let's tell all the experts to shut up."

Fancy looked concerned. "Did they give you a hard time at JANO?"

I nodded, too sad to spell it out.

"What did Edgar say?"

I mumbled. "He said I had to be nice to men."

Well, that really riled up Fancy. She turned and looked at the silly five who were listening to our conversation and gave them the Mafia Finger—a special hand job Fancy learned in the ghetto when she was doing the kind of social services work she had formerly believed in before she decided that the media was going to save the world.

They formed a defensive cluster and began talking about whether Mr. Ishmael still had his former energy and whether they should shop in his boutique.

Fancy and I pulled our chairs close as she went into serious matters. "Be nice to men? Ugh! They'll step all over you. Got to keep the battle going. It's the only chance we have to be happy."

At this point, the happy couple, Bitsy and Ernest, decided to treat everyone to the spectacle of watching them soul-kiss. She had to bend very far down to reach his open mouth, so much so that when he put his arms around her, it looked as if he were patting her flat ass. Actually, he was.

I knew what came next. The tossing of the bridal bouquet, which I expected to be an ugly squall. Fancy and I tried to wait it out, but our tablemates turned aggressively friendly, pushing us to center stage.

"Come on! We're the only single women here."

So—out on the floor we stood, the SHAMED SEVEN UNMARRIEDS!

(Was it possible that every other woman in the place was married? Wasn't anyone divorced?)

Frenzied screams.

Bitsy looked *veree* haughty as she raised her now-battered (courtesy of Ernest's kiss and ass-patting) wedding bouquet.

I stood there and watched it fly. Damn it! Was it coming at me?

It was.

The entire WASP tribe applauded as Bitsy pointed a bony finger at me and mouthed the words, "You're next!"

Yes. Yes. Yes.

I heard the "Wedding March" as clear as a bell. I saw the shining faces of wedding guests turn to me with happy expressions. Ahead was an altar, a priest, the golden vessels and tons of white roses.

Standing off to one side was the groom.

I squinted to see who it was.

Was it Harry?

Or was it my Darling Lad?

Was anybody there???

"Hey! Come back to earth, Lizzie." Fancy suggested with a disgusted look on her face. "Shall we retire to the Club Room?"

— 4 —

THE LOBBY'S CLUB ROOM is very clubby, with lots of tiny lamps and plenty of men. The waiters are on the watch for *the ladies of the night* and often refuse to seat two unescorted females.

Here's where being a media person counts. I was a fixture here because of my frequent lunches with hustling film publicists.

Henri spotted me, stared at Fancy's outfit, looked askance at the battered bouquet, and then sneered in that most eloquent way Frenchmen have—promptly shoving us towards a rear table. Fancy wasn't having this. She simply ignored him and walked over to a table close to a window overlooking the curbside—also endowed with a nice cross breeze from the men seated alone at the bar.

Henri huffed and puffed as I sneaked him a twenty. Not enough for good old Henri, who huffed and puffed some more.

"Oh, get lost, *Henry*," Fancy said, her voice rising.

I signaled Henri he'd better leave us be. He got the message.

As soon as our drinks arrived—Pellegrino for both of us, because we had serious things to talk about—I poked at the bouquet. "Does this mean I'm getting married?"

"Hey, you were really into it," Fancy said softly. "Are you turning into a bride?"

I shrugged. "My dad used to tell me that I didn't need the white dress."

"True enough." Fancy said nothing more. She knew any mention of my dad upset me.

"Still—Jane Austen always ends her books with a wedding. It's kind of nice."

That's when Fancy went into her rant. "Well, if you do what Edgar wants you to do, I'll order the invitations tomorrow. But remember—weddings are not the only criteria for Austen Girls. We want more than that."

"And that is?"

"We want to be in love forever and ever . . ."

"That's hard," I noted, then added, "Edgar said I should be *veree* civil to men."

"Does that mean you have to do everything they want?"

"I guess . . ."

"But you know how men are—Harry will want MUCH TOO MUCH SEX!"

"You think?"

"HOW MUCH SEX IS TOO MUCH SEX?" Fancy demanded.

I knew I was about to find out.

"Look, you can't give in to his sexual demands. Men are not like us. For them, sex is a get-hard-and-get-relief kind of thing."

"And for us?"

"It's OUR LIFE—isn't it? You can't give in to any peculiar thing he might want. My lord! He may even want you to cook."

"That's easy. I can always hire a cook or buy take-out."

"Yes, but you can't hire a bedmate for your sweetheart." She gave me an exasperated look as I opened my mouth. "Oh, no, Lizzie. Don't go there."

"Hey! I thought we were sexually free," I protested, though I was really just mouthing off.

Fancy gave me one of her don't-be-an-ass stares. "Mothers teach daughters—if you're really smart and want to keep your man, cook all his favorite foods in the kitchen and be his naughty girl in the bed."

I added, "And work and earn big bucks and drive the car and mow the lawn, even if you're having your period."

A moment of silence for our reverie, then Fancy got back into it. "Jane Austen really knows what the male of the species is all about."

"And that is?" I knew the answer but felt Fancy needed the line.

"Sometimes sweet. Often mean. Rarely delightful—after you give in to him. That's when he becomes an animal."

"And through it all I'm supposed to be a proper lady. Damn nonsense."

"Absolutely. But here's where you can use your up-to-now unfulfilled acting ability."

"Whot?"

"Shore up your Vanessa Redgrave soul. Smile and be so very pretty whilst telling Harry the lies he wants to hear."

"But that's what every other girl does. Aren't we JANO-ites different? Aren't we supposed to be truthful and have courage like Jane?"

"Hey, these days it takes a lot of courage to love a man the way Jane's girls did."

"With our whole hearts?"

Fancy shook her head and looked sooo sad, I had to say something *veree* courageous.

"Okay, I'll do it."

Surprised, her eyes sparkled with anticipation. "Do what?"

I took a long breath and went into it. "I'll be the sweetest, darlingest girl, who'll stroke Harry when he shows up for sex and love and any fetish that turns him on."

I giggled. "Then I'll turn him into my boytoy instead of treating him like a person."

Fancy brightened noticeably. "You mean the way men usually treat us?"

"Yes, and then some. For now, I'll forget about being a good Jane Austen person."

I turned my head so Fancy couldn't see my lips as I mouthed the words, *Forgive me, Jane.*

Fancy stared at me suspiciously, so I executed Mom's excuse for lying, the Sign of the Cross. At that, Fancy rolled her eyes and licked her lips, absolutely salivating.

"Oh, my. Poor Harry. I'm beginning to feel truly sorry for him. He's a *real* goner."

Chapter Eleven

— 1 —

WITHDRAWING FROM JANE AUSTEN was difficult, because my study paid homage to her. The smallish room sported a desk located between two floor-to-ceiling shuttered windows—the kind that always seemed to be featured in the sex scenes of European films. The windows overlooked the gardens behind Chez Gigi's kitchen, a French restaurant where scents of roasted meats from the ovens mixed with marijuana smoke from the staff to blast my senses every morning.

In cool contrast to this urban sin, my collection of Jane's novels in handsome leather editions lined the walls above my computer and three blowups of my fave author spanned the far wall. To be truthful, I didn't like the historical, official portrait of Jane. According to Austen lore, after Jane died, her sister Cassandra destroyed personal notes, letters, and sketches. For years there was no likeness of dear Jane. Later, when a sketch appeared with the claim that it was HERSELF, Austen fans (and publishers) were so desperate to have a portrait they devoured it.

As a result, this one sketch appeared in her books and

other paraphernalia. But there was one serious problem: Jane wasn't pretty.

The three sketches were hung side by side. The first was untouched (and ugly).

But the second was not. I'd begged my pal, Charles Von Kratt (the well-known artist) to tamper with it. But I told him to restrain himself. (Charles often signed his expensive canvases with smut, which he maintained raised their prices.)

Thanks to Charles' magic with pen and ink, Jane looked like a combination of Julianne Moore and Nicole Kidman in *The Hours*, a film I adored, though Charles did not include the infamous nose.

Okay. So the second copy was ladylike but prettier.

For the third copy, Charles volunteered to make Jane look sexy. I must admit I adore this version. Jane has a bosom, her bodice is torn, her mouth is suggestively open, and there's a *veree* hungry look in her eyes.

For me, this is the true Jane Austen. I believe sincerely that in her soul—Jane was *wild*.

Ah, these images were my gospel. Looking at them, I reached deep into my soul for truth and justice.

But now I had to banish them.

First, the books. I wrapped them in perfumed tissue paper, then heavy plastic, and placed them on a shelf in my hall storage closet. This meant that many New Balance shoes, tennis gear (oh, that was a while back), swim suits, a basket-ball (what was his name?), and stacks of magazines had to be shifted somewhere else.

I printed a large sign: Please Do Not Touch. On the odd chance that anyone went into my storage closet, they'd think these were pornographic books. (But Jane wouldn't know.)

Next, I used a ladder to unhook the first sketch, blew Jane

a kiss, and turned it around to see the United Poster price tag, $49.95, on the backing board.

When I turned the second, I found a message from Charles. "Lizzie, you have a great ass. Charles. 1996. NYC."

I was afraid to turn the last sketch around. If the classy transformation generated an ass compliment from Charles, what might I find on sexy Jane?

When I reversed the third sketch, my fears were realized as I read Charles' adieu. "Liz, babe. While you were in the shower, I blew off."

Blew off? Was that Charles' term for . . . ?

Yes, it was. There were unmistakable white stains on the backing board.

Ugh!

Semen in my study where I worked, read, and created—totally unaware that awful Charles had left an unsanitized gift!

Horrors!

I ran to the kitchen, got a towel and spray cleanser, went back, and rubbed, rubbed, rubbed (excuse the pun) the backing board. Hey, this stuff was stubborn. Back in the kitchen I found lemon juice and finally removed Charles' sperm from Jane's rear.

(Ooops, didn't mean to get vulgar.)

How dare Charles do this? I had a good mind to pick up the phone and tell him off. But Charles had become extremely successful and was married to the only female producer in Hollywood. Coward that I am, I planned to network her in the event I ever finished my damned screenplay.

Okay. Jane was out of my life. I felt desperate, depressed. I owe Jane Austen so much and wasn't sure I could live without her.

It was like losing a parent (which I knew about). Oh, don't go there, Lizzie. You have more to do.

– 2 –

THERE WAS ONLY ONE PERSON who could swiftly do the job—Adrienne, makeup artist to the stars and my mother's personal wardrobe adviser (which is why Mom walks around in skirts that showed off half her buttocks).

I phoned Adrienne, who'd just come in from an all-nighter working on a music video starring a teen too young to know that much about sex.

"Of course I'll help you, Lizzie baby."

"But you can't tell Mom."

"Honey, Maggie would *kvell* if she knew you were taking the right steps to become an attractive, metrosexual woman."

"A metrosexual woman?" This was a new one on me.

Adrienne was really excited. "I saw a show about metro-sexuality on Channel Four when I was in London last week. A metrosexual man paints his fingernails, braids his hair, and poses for sex magazines, but is a rigorous hetero."

"And what's a metrosexual woman?"

"The reverse. An M-woman wears low-slung jeans and cowboy boots, has lots of hair, and uses multiple products. She struts her stuff but is totally feminine in the sack while incorporating eternal, barefaced seduction tactics to stimulate and engage in SEX!"

Sounds like just what I needed.

"When can you come over?"

"I'm there already."

– 3 –

AT FIFTY-PLUS, ADRIENNE filled out her jeans as smashingly as she did when Mom first met her. In those days, Adrienne categorized females as babe/tart/shrew. Mom later plagiarized these terms for her book, *Why Women Are.*

This led to a terrible row and almost ended their friendship. But these galpals decided that absolutely nothing should erode what had taken women centuries to build. (Loyalty, I guess?)

Adrienne was fond of wearing T-shirts with one of her category labels. Today she wore a TART T-shirt. It was hot, and she'd rushed downtown so the shirt clung to her *veree* upright breasts so much that her large bosom seemed to be heaving.

These days she was a sizzling blonde. Cascades of golden hair fell in streams on her forehead and teased her patrician cheekbones and opalescent skin. Her body was quite voluptuous, and her T-shirt (below her ample tits) was torn at the bellybutton where she sported a red crystal stud.

Gawd, I thought, I'd like to be that sexy when I'm her age! Apparently, she read my thoughts, because Adrienne gave me a Tart smile, complete with wide mouth opened to reveal bright shiny teeth and a protruding pink tongue.

She said sternly, "Okay, you want to be seductive, and brilliant, and love men on your own terms. You have no need for marriage, which takes the romance out of a relationship."

"But . . ."

She shook her head. "The world doesn't revolve around romantic love. Nosiree. It's better to be a playful, wild, alive, intelligent woman."

"But that's the problem. Men don't seem to like that!"

She nodded. "Yes, they're quite stupid. They MUST BE TRAINED. If left on their own, they choose an organized woman who keeps the house, bakes cakes, and isn't too much trouble."

"Soooo—what do I do?"

"Easy. You're a warm and down-to-earth girl . . . sexy as hell. What you have to learn is how to be manipulative in a very organized, *mean* way."

"Huh?"

"It sounds bad, but it really isn't. It's fun, actually. You must play a role. You must be a courtesan. I will teach you how."

"Is it difficult?"

"No, because you are a complex person and truly wonderful."

I blushed. "And how do I play this?"

"You must totally analyze the man you wish to seduce. Here are the rules: ask him about his adolescence—when he first had sex, what he thought of it. Who was his turn-on? Remember—to seduce a man, you have to know him as a boy first. And if you succeed, he will become your boytoy, and you can do whatever you wish with him."

She laughed. "You must learn the rules. How to undress gracefully. How to peel a banana and swallow it without gagging. How to wear lacy lingerie to emphasize the way your bosom heaves. How to be very playful and nice to your man."

Suddenly, she looked sad. "But remember . . . if you turn out to be this kind of woman, all other women will hate you. Are you willing to take that risk?"

I felt unnerved. "Oh, no. My friends are too important to me."

Her eyes narrowed. "And how many girlfriends do you have, Lizzie? Not many, I'd wager."

"Well, there's Fancy, and . . ."

Hey, she was right. Many women in my life were Bitsy-type acquaintances, not real friends.

I mumbled, "Guess just one."

"Like me. Your mother is my true friend. We were both

abandoned by our husbands and decided to live our lives according to our own rules."

"Did Dietrich run out on you?" Dietrich was Adrienne's German director husband.

"Yes, he cut me to shreds. I was censored, edited, plundered, and left to die. That's how men were back then. They didn't leave you, they annihilated you."

I took a chance. "Is that what my father did?"

Adrienne answered honorably.

"Lizzie, I can't talk about your mom and dad. Only Maggie can tell you that story."

"But she won't," I complained.

— 4 —

ADRIENNE HELD UP A HAND for silence as she opened a gray satin tote. "All right. Let's start with your skin. We will cleanse, hydrate, and revitalize your face. I use thirty-seven different amino acids and pure oxygen gas for this. Then we'll do a body wrap with a mud mask, scrub your body with Dead Sea salts and soak your hair in a sea clay solution. After that, we will sip herbal tea or cider and let soft music take us away to a place of beauty. Then the real work begins."

"All this to get a man?"

(I couldn't believe I was willing to go through so much for a man. Where's my integrity? How can I live with myself?)

Undaunted, Adrienne continued. "My philosophy is beauty from the inside out. We take care of the outside, and then we meditate and take care of the inside. Your brain and soul control your body . . . your eroticism dwells deep within your body."

"And how do we know this will work?"

Her voice was hushed. "This is the metrosexual method. Products beget the soul, which begets the body, which begets pleasure."

"Wait a sec. Could you be more specific?"

"Well," she mused, "before you see your lover, we'll have a few trial runs."

What was she talking about? "Trial runs??"

"Yes, yes. Self-pampering." She had a silly look on her face. "Get what I mean?" she asked.

What was I getting myself into? What did metrosexual really mean? Then it became clear. I nodded at Adrienne with powerful understanding.

Yessirree. I got it.

Chapter Twelve

— 1 —

S O THERE I WAS—all plucked up like a sacrificial
chicken for Harry.

On my feet were flat sandals sporting a jeweled key-
chain—cost, $400.

Yipes!

But Adrienne had spent an hour smoothing my feet with
a pumice stone and insisted on my wearing the pricey
footwear. She'd also erased my pesky crow's-feet using a tube
of Sparkle-spackle while remarking that I was much too
young to have them.

And that wasn't all. Adrienne choose a pair of blue short-
shorts, matching them with a revealing top.

When I commented that this outfit seemed a bit pedes-
trian, she explained that it was always best to look casual
when your lover expected hot sex.

"Voila!" She exclaimed, handing me blue sequined fashion
frames.

Confronted with my reflection, I felt silly. "I look like an
idiot."

Of course Adrienne had a response. "Lizzie, I bought those frames in Paris."

Ever the fashion maven, to Adrienne, Paris fell somewhere between Mecca and Heaven. I still felt stupid, though. "Okay. But they really don't match this idiot naval outfit."

Rapidly, she shook her head. I think she was a bit exasperated. "Just think of yourself as a mermaid—half woman, half primitive. Your buttocks are your tail, and you can whip them around at will. That'll give you a great source of fluidity and power . . . but it will not offend your man—he won't really know where it's coming from."

Mermaid? Me?

I thought of all those films where a sea nymph captures the heart of the handsome captain, downs his ship, and beckons him into the sea for eternity. Of course there were the reverse stories, where the captain beckons the mermaid to earth, and she flops about with that giant tail, requiring her suitor to have a large bathtub.

I felt like arguing and knew what would do it. "So what's the difference between a courtesan and a hooker?" I inquired snidely.

A total Francophile, she rolled her eyes. "*Mon Dieu!* It's like wine and water." Adrienne cleared her throat. "How shall I begin? Okay. For a courtesan, love is a mysterious force with vast power over her life to which she must fiercely comply. For her, saying no to love is tragic."

"But when does this romance stuff become pathology?" I switched to my best journalistic interrogation technique.

Adrienne's affectations disappeared as she grew silent. For this fifty-plus lady, being ever optimistic about love was akin to surviving life. While I, on the other hand, thought that love tended to be a short-lived phenomenon.

It seems to me that the longer the affair, the more difficult things get. The first part is okay. We shag at my house, order take-out, and go to films.

But things changed when we began staying at Gabe's place. I *couldn't* go out for a walk without telling him exactly where I was going. I *couldn't* close the bathroom door, just in case he needed to pee. I *couldn't* eat breakfast in bed, because crumbs fell on the mattress. I *couldn't* shave my legs and armpits, because Gabe felt hair was "erotic." I *couldn't* have an ice cream sundae, a specialty of the hotel kitchen. And I *couldn't* order tofu from the Chinese restaurant.

And the morning he found me standing next to his computer, he went into a rage, accusing me of infringing on his privacy. That's when I left, unwilling to spend one more minute with this obsessive-compulsive maniac.

Sure, Gabe was great in the sack and good to look at. But the rest of it was sheer madness.

Bad things always happen when I stay at a man's place . . . never at mine. At my place, Gabe was polite, nice, sweet, and very complimentary.

Now, Harry was an ardent romantic. But I'd never been to Harry's place. If I was going to try this courtesan skirmish, that would be the test.

— 2 —

I WALKED ALONG BLEECKER STREET and thought of Mom's tales of a community of coffeehouses, bookshops, cheap apartments, and friendly neighbors. Aside from Paris, France, Mom felt there was no place that tolerated sexual freedom, radical politics, offbeat philosophies, and all sorts of hustling mavericks than this part of the world.

Now that was gone. The streets became a haven for tourists: plump women, men, and children with ice cream in one hand and pizza in another, who, too late, wanted to catch the vanished avant-garde.

I zigzagged along crowded, tiny streets until I reached Commerce Street, a thoroughfare lined with brownstones and orange blossom trees. In the middle of the block, in a three-story townhouse resided dear Harry.

He was one of the lucky ones. His mother, an off-Broadway actress, bought the place in the Fifties before he was born. He'd confided that the mortgage was paid, the garden was lovely, and he had no intention of renting any part of it out.

Lucky Harry. What did he do with so much space? Well—I was about to find out. I ran up the stairs. There was no intercom, but the door sported a brass knocker. When I used it, a lace curtain moved. I guess Harry's method of checking visitors was peeking through the window.

Shades of Jane Austen!

— 3 —

AT THE DOOR, HARRY wore new pajama bottoms of grey silk. I wondered whether he was alone. When he looked me up and down and said, "Wow! Come on in!" I decided this was not going to go like Bridget finding that American tart in Daniel Cleaver's flat.

I walked into a countrified atmosphere. The place seemed like a New England barn, all brick walls and wide beams looking as if they'd been carved from New Hampshire trees. The woody motif continued with a wide coffee table piled high with books, CDs, and photographs. I guess Harry was working.

The fireplace was gorgeous, bricks arranged in a herringbone design I'd never seen before. Above it hung a poster for *La Dolce Vita* in the original Italian. It was obviously part of a costly collection.

Before I could check out the others, Harry took my arm and said, "Let's go out to the solarium."

Here, the countrified feeling continued. Wicker chairs and couches, plants of every size and description, a humongous fish tank, a woven floor rug, and darling throw pillows in warm colors—gold, tangerine, and lilac.

Veree lovely!

Ordinarily I'd ask Harry who did the charming interiors, but this was not a normal rendezvous. He offered wine and as we sipped, true to my courtesan responsibilities, I asked him how I could please him.

He looked odd. "Huh?"

I began. "I know I'm fickle with men. You've probably heard all the stories."

He nodded.

Hmmm. What had he heard?

I pursued my task. "I know what I want in a man." I gave him an intense eye tease (Adrienne's specialty).

His voice grew hoarse. "Lizzie, you're so hot. At the office, that's all I hear."

"What do you hear?"

"That you're the hottest woman on *The Record.*"

Guess he didn't know about Fancy, whose record with men was even more undisciplined than mine.

I said quickly, "Look, I'm a simple girl. I like sipping cappuccino in a café. I like to walk around the Village. I like *all* Italian restaurants, northern and southern. And, as you know, I'll go to films at the drop of a hat."

I sighed wisely (I hoped). "Films are my life." I waited for his response.

"That's your job . . ." he said rather officiously.

Was he being the boss?

Don't know how it happened, but my mood turned around from courtesan to cantankerous crank.

"Harry, why are you dressed in pajamas at three o'clock in the afternoon? Did someone just leave your bed? Maybe Sherry?"

His voice grew hoarse. "Are you going to do it again?"

I tried to look innocent. "What again?"

"Don't pretend you don't know the effect you have when you act jealous. You really turn me on."

Harry leaned back in his chair and stared. I was excited but underneath felt something was wrong.

"Damn it. You excite me, Lizzie!" He pulled me to him. When he kissed me, his tongue pushed deeply into my dry mouth. I felt sick to my stomach, the way I always feel during airplane takeoffs.

When our lips parted, I whispered, "Have you done it with her?"

"Yes, this morning. I did Sherry. Did her good, she said."

My world closed in. What the hell! Another cheat!!!

I pushed him away. "You son of a bitch!"

Looking startled, he countered, "Look, you wanted me— then you didn't want me, and I didn't like how you made me feel."

I walked the plank—in this case from wall to wall. "Sure, blame it on me," I retorted.

"But we didn't have an exclusive." He grabbed me again and whispered, "What are you wearing under those tiny shorts?"

I hated him. "Don't touch me."

He released me so fast, I stumbled and grabbed the arm of a chair in the nick of time.

"Tart!" he accused.

"Cheat!" I retaliated.

Boy! Harry grabbed me, and we were off and running. I tried to remember my courtesan lessons and do the things Adrienne taught me. They seemed to work. Harry touched me in the oddest places. I was enjoying it all when I spotted the film poster on one wall.

What the hell! I stopped Harry in mid-foreplay.

"Excuse me a second."

"What?" He sounded angry.

I hopped over to the poster, took it down, and lovingly placed it against the wall next to the fireplace. As I turned it, I kissed my Darling Lad's image on the lips. "Sorry. This is how it has to be for now. But I'll be back."

"So there you are," Harry said, lying on the couch naked, looking a bit like Oliver Reed in the male nude scene from *Women in Love*. (Unfortunately, they cut this *veree* sexy scene when they released it worldwide. Quite annoying. It was a great scene for ladies. Hot stuff.)

"Okay. Let's get on with it," I said.

He looked a bit strange but was caught up in the moment. And then the next one.

Several hours later we sat on the couch, drinking champagne, satiated with sex and caring—the way those French actors in all Louis Malle films always seem. I realized this courtesan business was quite remarkable. I learned so much. Before today, I didn't know men could have multiple orgasms, too.

Then Harry said, "What's with you, Lizzie?"

I beamed. "Did you love it?"

"I'm not sure. You're not the Lizzie I know."

"A sexier Lizzie?"

He looked puzzled. "No one is sexier than *my* sweet Lizzie."

Uh-oh. What was this about?

"But you had three orgasms!" He nodded. Then why did he look so unhappy? "Isn't that what men want?"

Harry pulled me close. "Hey, I'm not *men*. I'm Harry. Remember me?"

Then he reminded me that he was Harry one more time.

After his fourth big O (this is hard to believe—could it be some kind of record?) Harry looked sober.

"Ron is thinking of ending his marriage."

Okay. This was the time after sex where secrets are revealed. So why are we talking about the boss?

I remained calm. "After all those years and all those children?"

"Yes, he's simply mad for Sherry."

Silence . . . then . . .

"Does he know you shagged her?" I asked.

"No."

I sat upright, unable to contain myself.

"So you really *did* shag her!!" I screamed.

I bounced out of his arms, noting however that he was in the state of firmness again.

"Oh, don't make such a big thing about it. We hadn't taken any vows. Haven't yet—have we?"

"What vows?"

"The 'we are going steady' vows, the 'I'll see you every Saturday and Sunday' vows."

I exploded. "If you think you're going to have carte blanche with me while you screw around—"

"Shag," he interrupted. "I thought you liked shag better."

"*Shag* about with every film star who comes your way and doesn't have a date—well, can it."

"What if I told you I love you? I do, you know."

"As if—" I snorted.

That did it. He jumped to his feet and confronted me. "What more do you fucking *want*?"

"I want to smell it—I want to see it—I want to feel it—"

"Feel what?"

"Love—I want to feel love." I burst into tears. "I want to know it's true."

"It's true all right." Harry kissed me tenderly. "There—do you feel it now?"

"Almost . . . only almost."

He stared at me, his eyes slit like a serial killer's in a bad film. Then he raised his hands in a helpless gesture, as if he were alone in the middle of the ocean and needed rescue.

"Hell, Lizzie—what do I have to do to prove that I care?"

"*Care?* You said love."

He croaked, "Lizzie, I adore you, but you're making all this too hard . . . besides, you've been faking it all afternoon."

I gasped.

"Didn't you think I'd know when my girl wasn't really getting it?" he said.

"I—I—"

He looked at me sadly. "Fuck!!" he said and left the room. A few minutes later, I heard him going upstairs.

I sat there for a moment, trying to decide what to do. Should I run after Harry and say I was sorry? I knew what was wrong. I'd performed well, but I wasn't true to myself.

I felt a little bit tipsy, picked up my shorts, my panties with *Lizzie baby* embroidered on them, the matching bra with the words *sexy bitch*, my very wrinkled top, and my Hermes bag from which a remarkable supply of condoms had exploded.

Hey! I'd performed as a courtesan, had GREAT SEX, and still felt like a failure.

Ugh!

This whole experience was really gross!

My silly life was falling apart. I didn't know that as a courtesan I'd lose my orgasms.

Harry was correct. All my sounds throughout the afternoon, I'm sorry to say, were purely fake. I sounded like a simpering, silly soprano (no, not the killers—the ones who sing).

Apparently Harry is a Sherlock Holmes of eroticism. He kept asking me questions in a *veree* suspicious manner.

Did you really come?
My god, why are you screaming like that?
Christ, are you having a heart attack?

And I said, as winningly as I could, "Oh, no. It's you, Harry.

"You're just F A B U L O U S !"

— 4 —

MORAL LESSON

FAKING SEX SIMPLY DOESN'T WORK!
IT'S MUCH BETTER TO BE
UN-ORGASMIC—
UN-ERECTED—
UN-REQUITED—
AT LEAST YOU *FEEL*—
PERFORMANCE SEX IS STUPID!

But it seems popular. No wonder the world is in such a bad state of affairs—love affairs, I mean.

But I couldn't save the *whole world*.

Dear Jane would say I must examine my situation.
So . . .

Was Harry in love with me?
He didn't act as if he were.
But then—
How does a man in love act?

I simply didn't know.

Chapter Thirteen

$\mathcal{CSO}$

— 1 —

HOME AT LAST, I popped the video of *Pride and Prejudice* in the VCR. I felt like Elizabeth Bennet when she encountered Darcy's Pemberly estate for the first time. "And of this place . . . I might have been mistress!" she muses. Even at ten (when I originally read *Pride and Prejudice*), I knew Elizabeth would marry Darcy after seeing his terrific home.

And right this minute, I wanted to move into Harry's elegant townhouse with its lovely garden on a quiet street. But unlike Elizabeth, who'd declined Darcy's marriage offer—so she had a heads-up—Harry wasn't offering me anything except weekend shags.

Yes, he said he loved me. But he didn't act as if he did. I simply didn't know how to get him to commit. And—commit to what?

Why wasn't I as smart as Elizabeth Bennet? I'd spent the better part of the last two days learning how to bend, manipulate, and excite Harry—to have him still walk out on me. Though our shagging got hotter and hotter, we weren't nice to each other at all. We became two mean people doing weird stuff and fighting over nonsense.

How did I become this girlfriend unable to cope with men, chocolate, and prime bachelor Harry Archer?

What the hell was wrong with me?

I knew the answer. This courtesan stuff wasn't working for me because Jane Austen wouldn't release me from her rules. From a perch in literary heaven, she'd given me a dispensation to take part in film business double-dealing.

But during the last forty-eight hours, I'd committed a really serious sin:

I'd forgotten what it was to be an Austen Girl!!!

Time to make amends.

I went into the study and released Jane's sketches from purgatory. In the kitchen, I chose the teapot I'd bought at the Tea & Sympathy shop on Greenwich Avenue. I spooned in Fortnum and Mason tea as I waited for the kettle to boil.

Holding a cup of delicate china and sipping the tea transported me back into Jane's time. I became one of the Dashwood sisters, sitting next to the pianoforte on a lazy summer afternoon, neighbors playing cricket on the lawn, a country picnic about to begin. Conversation flowed over tea, a bit of gossip about another family, a naughty anecdote.

It was a time when men and women cherished each other . . .

That's what I wanted.

But it wasn't to be—not with Harry.

Instead, my thoughts returned to my Darling Lad.

Right now he's only on celluloid. But next month, he'd arrive in Gotham to publicize his latest film.

That's when my life would get on track. For I was invited to the Metro Film Festival, where I would finally meet my darling.

− 2 −

I MUST HAVE FALLEN ASLEEP, but I woke up weary. The phone was ringing. I picked it up to hear Tony Palermo's trembling voice.

I'd been neglecting Tony in my pursuit of the love of Harry Archer, so I hoped this wasn't going to be one of those "you never have time for me anymore" conversations.

"Look, Lizzie, I hate to do this."

I played stupid. "Do what?"

At first, he hemmed and hawed, then finally blurted, "I need your press pass."

Why did *The Record*'s public relations manager need my sacred press pass? "Whatever for?"

"The boss wants it back."

I brightened. "Am I getting a new one?"

"Lizzie, I hate to tell you this. Ron says he needs more versatility in the film reviews."

"Ron? You mean Harry?"

"Well, both," he fudged.

"Are you saying I've lost my gig?"

"Don't get upset, Lizzie. Promise me you won't go out and get annihilated on martinis the way you did when you found out I wouldn't have sex with you."

What was he talking about? Hell, men were something else. "Tony, we've always been great pals."

"Yeah. Yeah."

A pause, then, "Look, you'll connect with another rag soon. You're so good. And you have a good rep."

I realized then and there that Tony was feeling truly neglected, but I didn't have time to stroke him.

"Tony, be honest. Has my shagging Harry had anything to do with this?"

"Uh, maybe . . . indirectly."

"Please explain."

"I don't know for certain. But I know that I have to get your press pass back, and I feel shitty."

This public relations guru knew all there was to know about Manhattan's dirty secrets so I asked him, "Can I bring Harry up on sex-harassment charges?"

"Bring him up where? You're not on staff, you're a freelancer. Your editor has a right to have your press pass returned at any time."

Tony took another call, then returned to say, "You have no legal rights, because you have no contract. Also, if you do this, who's going to hire a troublemaker?"

Tony ranted, "Furthermore, what would you charge him with? You wanted to shag him, didn't you?"

Right!

What could I charge Harry with?

Tony continued his diatribe. "Anyhow, I don't think it was Harry. I think Sherry had you fired."

"Why would she do that?"

"Sherry knows Harry likes you, and Ron adores Sherry."

"Doesn't Ron know she's shagging Harry?"

"Maybe yes and maybe no." He lowered his voice. "But I think the bitch did the dirty deed."

"Then I have no recourse except to do her bodily harm."

Visions exploded. Tearing the bimbo's fake red tresses out by the roots. Smashing her pert plastic-surgery nose flat. Kicking her right in the vagina—where I knew it would hurt plenty.

Tony burst my pipe dream. "But that wouldn't be professional, would it? Hey, aren't you the one who keeps on saying you don't want to be the girl? Well, take your medicine like a man."

"Ugh," I grunted.

"You're a professional, aren't you, Lizzie?"

Yes, I was.

And that made me feel truly impotent.

The truth is, I like being a media celebrity. I like being part of this tawdry, glittery, superficial crowd who attend film screenings and attempt to say things that might sound intelligent in print about film stars.

I admit it. I'm guilty of a psychological obsession called . . . *CELEBRITY ADDICTION.*

The Celebrity Addict's Six-Step Identification Program:

Step 1: identification with a celebrity on a social and professional level

Step 2: identifying on a personal level—empathizing about a star's life as if he were a close pal

Step 3: becoming totally absorbed by the star and wanting a relationship

Step 4: sending him notes and letters

Step 5: stalking him

Step 6: moving to his neighborhood

Already I was guilty of Steps 1 through 3. But my excuse was that it was part of my job—I was a film critic, wasn't I?

The question was—for how long?

My hands shook as I took my press pass from my bag. This is my passport to sanity.

I *need* it.

Have to have it.

I *must* remain a full-fledged professional scribe, where it's okay to obsess about my Darling Lad.

If I wasn't media—I could become a stark, raving stalker, couldn't I?

How the hell did all this happen? I used to be a sweet girl who loved her father and her mother, her TV programs, her films, her hobbies, her life!

But then came the time when there was only Mom. After Dad left, she'd really climbed on her political bandwagon and never got off.

When Dad was home, I'd hear them arguing about me.

"Lizzie has a right to feel her life is going to be happy. She's got a right to dream her dreams."

"That's for brainless kids. My Lizzie has to learn the truth about life."

"She's mine, too, Maggie."

My mother's voice was suddenly brimming with anger. "You're not home enough. You have no say—none at all. And remember, Lizzie comes first."

My mother expected too much of me and let me know it every minute of every day. She'd say, "Look, Lizzie, no one else will tell you the truth. Everybody lies. Trust no one. Only me."

With that attitude, I grew up an emotional mess. Yes, I blame her. She freaked out my dad until he finally had to leave us.

Still, while Mom was hard to take, she was always there. And Dad wasn't.

Maybe it was time for me to be realistic about Dad. I went into the bedroom, removed his photograph from my bedside, and stuck it behind the *Encyclopedia Britannica* on the bottom bookshelf.

I felt really weird, as if I'd lost Dad for a second time.

But I told myself, Lizzie, you've got to get it. Your Dad isn't here for you.

But your Mom is.

And I needed to see her.

— 3 —

I ENTERED MY mother's Tribeca loft with my key since there was no answer on the intercom. The phones were ringing (she had two separate phones—no call waiting for dear Maggie).

The place had the appearance of a party about to happen anywhere in the world. On one wall a clock marked *Paris* hung above a drafting table laden with costume sketches.

On the opposite wall, another clock marked *London* kept time above a John Chamberlain crashed cab, circa 1967—the year Mom met Dad.

Because she loved to cook, Mom spent major money on the kitchen. It was spacious and housed a collection of two dozen copper pots.

The kitchen sink was gray marble and could easily be identified as the good-sized bathtub it originally was. And Mom's collection of Chinese porcelain plates was displayed on the pale walls alongside two huge paintings of the Madonna and Child.

Above a cast iron stove hung a printed set of household rules.

Chez Maggie

1. Pay special attention to all guests, especially eligible ones
2. Arrange bouquets of flowers in large vases

3. Serve fruits and vegetables in season
4. Allow no children, pets, or married couples to
dine here
5. Serve only wine, no other beverage is available at
Chez Maggie

In keeping with her last rule, crystal glassware stood proudly displayed on triangular shelves set in a corner, looking very much like little toy soldiers arrayed to do battle—and perhaps they were!

I walked down the hall to a smallish space Mom liked to call the *Room of Remembrances.*

A faded model of a doll house stood against a wall surrounded by a potpourri of photographs of my family—hot women, all.

Head shots of Alice in her prime; landscape shots of Maggie in the summer, wearing long, floral dresses which always reminded me of Austen clothes.

And shots of me: a curly-blond Botticelli baby; a serious, wide-eyeglassed scholar; a budding, cropped-hair-and-jeans teen; finally THE HOT LADY I AM TODAY!!

It was a deeply moving visual essay about my family—where no men existed.

I shouldn't invade Mom's privacy while she was out, but I went into her bedroom anyway. Her vanity table supported a cosmetics explosion. Dozens of bottles of foundation makeup, trays of rouges, lip gloss, eye shadow, mascaras, pencils, and beauty spots.

There was a pile of freebie coupons distributed by cosmetic companies at film launches and publicity parties. Clairol, Revlon. Lord—even Maybelline.

I shook my head in disbelief. Why was Mom so obsessed with makeup? She certainly didn't need it.

In contrast to the vanity, the closet was neat and spare. Four short skirts. Three evening skirts. Five pair of pants. A dozen tops. Two coats. Four pair of shoes. Seven handbags. Nothing very interesting.

In a corner of the room, Mom had set up a small desk for letters and bills. She must have been in a hurry, because it was messy with mail, newspaper clips, and a variety of colored pens.

I felt uncomfortable rummaging around Mom's personal papers and decided to take off. That's when I saw that the wall safe was open.

I knew I shouldn't, but I slid my hand inside the safe. There was a bunch of legal papers—probably Mom's will, a deed to the apartment, insurance, stuff that wasn't interesting to me.

I felt along the edge of the safe. There was something more. Perhaps there were letters from Dad, or information about why he'd left. Maybe even a letter with his address.

I found a box filled with notebooks. I sat on the edge of the bed and read through them. They were the usual writer's notes about places Mom visited, observations jotted down, household chores, phone numbers, business appointments.

The last notebook was a bit tattered. Dated 1979, the year of Dad's departure, the first pages were filled with comments about her daughter—me. Mom was very worried about how I would cope without a father.

The middle section was filled with her poetry. I read through them—all testimonials of her love for Dad.

When I read the last entry, I wept.

I struggle alone in the dark
My beloved Lizzie is sleeping
We must stay alive for each other

Chapter Fourteen

— 1 —

MY MOUTH WAS DRY. I felt as if my world was evaporating into a pool of tears as I reread the lines of Mom's poems.

These words told me that underneath my mother's political rhetoric was a sad, emotional woman who was terribly scared. That's why she pontificated at me—she was hiding her own terrors about life.

Here was evidence that Mom was devoted to me all the while she'd proselytized about men's faults, proclaiming how a girl like me had a duty to become a feminist heroine.

Her life was a total sham, a magnificent performance.

Only Mom was not on the stage. She lived in my heart and in my head.

And this behavior had influenced my own life choices.

I could not dismiss her deception, for I had my own. While Mom hid behind political rhetoric, I camouflaged my own fears using humor and sophisticated chatter about men, sex, and the entire industry known as filmmaking.

So far, it hadn't worked too well for me—though I was working at improving.

And it hadn't worked for Mom—that's why she had that

makeup obsession . . . spending hours before her vanity, inventing an artificial Maggie—hiding the deeply passionate woman who was at odds with her feminist theories.

But could she change at this late date? My own maturity was still evolving, and I had Jane Austen and the JANO-ites to keep me on the straight and narrow path to honesty and sincerity.

I shut the notebook and put it in the box, then placed everything back in the safe. I returned to the kitchen and thought about how to be generous to Mom instead of flinching at every word she pronounced.

But could I? I'd been on the receiving end of her criticism for so many years that my response was automatic.

Could I stop the flow of sophisticated rebuttals that had become my pattern? I knew I couldn't do it one hundred percent—Jane Austen's irony was one of my coping tools. But I could try to be more compassionate to my mom. She needed my love and friendship.

But it had to be as woman to woman. We could no longer be mother and child.

– 2 –

I HEARD SOUNDS AT THE DOOR and quickly put a smile on my face. After a couple of minutes of fumbling with her key, my mother entered.

"Lizzie, darling! What are you doing here?"

"Came to see you," I said sincerely.

"Yeah, I'll bet. Need money?"

"No, Mom."

"Okay. Then let's start the fashion show."

She rolled in a carryall and unzipped it to show me her new gear. Since I routinely describe Mom's outfits as "odd", I wasn't particularly astonished to see a feathered turban, a crisp bikini sashed with polka-dot bows, a tweed skirt decorated with sequins—nor a gray organza dress with gauzy layers of lace and chiffon throughout, which had practically no bodice and was *veree* short.

I wondered if Mom was going into menopause and whether she should see a doctor as she preened in front of a mirror, fluffed her hair, and said, "I simply don't know what to wear."

"Going someplace special?"

Her eyelids crinkled. "They're screening *The Festival* at six. Want to come with me?"

"*The Festival*? Never heard of it."

She gave me a lopsided smile. "It's my nudie film."

Lizzie, remember your resolutions.

Calmly, I put on the tea kettle and began arranging a tray with cups, saucers, spoons, napkins, teapot, and tea. Under my breath, I murmured, "Jane Austen, keep me sane. Please, Jane, get me through the next hour."

That's what was so nice about Jane—you could always count on her for support.

"Well, do you want to come?"

"Mom? Do you think you're going through menopause?" I asked.

"What does that mean?"

"Remember your book *Why Women Are*? You did all that research about hormones and women?"

She nodded but retained a suspicious air.

"Well, everything I've read lately proves the unfathomable fact that passionate women, more than passive women, are slaves to their hormonal swings. And everyone knows what a hot lady you are."

It was probably the wrong thing to say. My words seemed to choke me, and I couldn't continue.

But Mom was composed. "I don't believe in all that hormonal stuff any longer. While it's true that men are complete slaves to their fiendish desires to hump and hunt, women aren't."

"So . . . you're okay about this film?"

"I haven't seen it, so I don't know if it's any good."

"I mean, are you okay being nude?"

"Anything not to wear a bra."

This must be a private joke, because Mom giggled like a teenager.

Just then the kettle whistled. I searched the tea stash and decided that only sweet, soothing mint would do for what was coming. With trembling hands I poured the boiling water into the teapot and carried the tray to the round Formica table where Mom liked to breakfast.

Hanging plants, two birdcages (sans birds) and Matisse prints on the wall redeemed the fact that the area was really too small for two people.

I sat on the cane chair facing Mom. "I don't get it . . ." I mumbled.

She raised both her hands and examined her impeccably manicured fingers. "Hmmm. Maybe I should wear that plunging black halter dress that shows my fuchsia bra straps—the ones that match my open-toe heels. I could paint my toenails to match too, couldn't I?"

"Mom!!" So help me—I sounded a bit stern.

Her face took on a hyper-enthusiastic expression. "Let me tell you all about me and sex, Lizzie. You're old enough."

I wasn't sure anyone was old enough to hear this from her

mother. But I told myself to think of Mom as a friend, not a parent.

"Okay," I said, pouring the tea for us and praying to Jane yet again.

— 3 —

TEARS RAN DOWN MOM'S cheeks, but she was smiling as well. "I lost my virginity under the entrance to the George Washington Bridge."

"How old were you?" I croaked.

"Fifteen," she replied.

I wanted to glorify this romantic event. "So you fell in love!"

Mom shook her head. "Love had nothing to do with it. In fact, I didn't even like the boy."

"Then why?"

For a moment, her expression went blank, then she looked at me as if assessing my response before springing her accusation. "It was your grandmother's fault."

"Gran told you to have sex?"

"Not exactly."

Critically she eyed her teacup. Mom hated Jane Austen, claiming she was too prissy. Still, I was hoping she'd partake of the calming tea.

No chance. She rose from the chair, went over to the cupboard, located a bottle of Haig & Haig Scotch, and filled a tumbler glass. In one gulp, half was gone.

Now her cheeks grew flushed. "I know you don't approve, Lizzie. But some habits die hard."

I tried to get her back on track. "So what happened—with sex, I mean?"

Like a sultry songstress between takes, she cleared her throat. When she continued speaking her voice had gone at least an octave south. Maybe there was a benefit to Scotch whiskey, after all.

Easily Mom escalated the drama of her tale. "When I was fourteen I had no bosom. Then I turned fifteen and in a few months my breasts grew so much that when I went to shoot baskets, I found myself bouncing more than the ball. Miss Everhard, the gym instructor, told me I had to wear a bra. I refused. Remember, these were radical times, and burning bras was a symbol of women's independence. I had read the feminists about bonding and so on.

"So Miss E. sent a note to Gran, who was furious. Remember how much her corsets meant to her? The next day Gran marched me down to the Lower East Side and the store that custom-made her naughty ones."

Mom picked up the glass of Scotch. I swear she gargled it before she drank it.

Then . . . "When we walked in I was a free spirit, a young woman of promise with her future ahead of her. When we walked out, I was in pain and despair."

"From a fitting?"

"Yes. Mrs. Glickstein was harsh. She gave a couple of thumps on my hips and buttocks, put her arms around my waist, and squeezed hard. Then she did the same at my chest and in a thick accent announced I was a C cup. Imagine!! A couple of months ago I was flat, and now this *Yiddishe Mama* is telling me that I skipped over A and B, straight to C? No way."

She took a deep breath and coughed some more. "But Gran believed Mrs. G. so I had to try on a dozen bras. After watching with an eagle eye, Gran decided Maidenform held me in the most. Damn! Fifteen years old and learning about the facts of a woman's life firsthand."

"Didn't they have sexy ones?" I asked, thinking of the uplift French bra under my shirt—the one with the embroidered hands cupping the nipples.

"Apparently not. And that wasn't the end of it. Mrs. G. also brought out garter belts, girdles, waist cinchers, even a corset like Gran used. She said I was hard to fit because my breasts were already sagging."

"What?" I sipped the tea too fast and burned my tongue. Quickly, I ran to the sink and splashed cold water on it.

I was still bent over when my mother pronounced in tones of doom, "You're right to be frightened, Lizzie. Apparently it's in our genes."

Surreptitiously, I touched my breasts. They seemed to be okay. No sagging. I tried to relax as Mom continued.

"The whole experience was scary. As soon as I saw the frayed pink curtain in the dressing room behind the cash register I thought, *what is Mom thinking of? Why doesn't she shop for naughty French stuff at Bergdorf-Goodman?* She had the money, for heaven's sake."

"Did you ask her?"

Mom nodded. "She said bra fitting is an art, and only married women from a certain section of Vienna are good at it." Mom shook her head. "That was Gran. She always knew where to go to get the best stuff."

She coughed, tried to sip her tea, but gagged. After a brief struggle to regain her composure, she continued, "Gran said, 'This is the first day of the rest of your life. You will come here to Mrs. G. always. It is our lifetime commitment to the Glickstein family.'"

"Oh, Gawd."

Dramatically, Mom tossed back her long hair. "Yes, Lizzie,

I was trapped. In those days, girls were terrified of their moms. Not like now."

She punctuated that remark with a pointed glance at me. "I did protest, though. I told Gran that we stood at the dawn of a New Age, where women were not going to be trussed up like chickens and served to the first available man for marriage, bearing children, and all of that."

"Did she buy that?"

"Nope. She said, 'Why would you think I'd wish that misery for you? But that has nothing to do with bra etiquette.' I unfortunately answered, 'Screw that!' Your grandmother's response was a stiff slap to my face. Hard."

"Gran?" I was shocked.

"She never did it again. As you know, I have *never* disciplined you that way." I nodded thankfully.

"I was hurt and ran out of the dressing room. That's when I saw Mrs. G. patting down a tall transsexual who was fingering a blue velvet corselet, much like the one Gran wore. I was so surprised that I stared impolitely. Gran said, 'What's wrong with you? Haven't you ever seen a female impersonator before?' At which point the elegant transsexual screamed, 'I am *not* a female impersonator—I am a *female*! Want to see?' He began to unzip his skirt."

I let out a loud laugh. "Oh, hell. That's game."

Mom sounded a little diva-y. "Oh, yes. It was 1963, and the Lower East Side supplied every entertainer in the city. Right then, though, most of Mrs. Glickstein's customers were married ladies. When they heard this threat, they took off, yelling, 'This isn't *his* day.'"

"What did they mean?"

"Apparently, there were rules. On Tuesdays, the crossdressers came. On Wednesdays, the transsexuals. But this was Thursday, when ordinary women could shop. This girl/guy had gotten his dates wrong."

"Sounds pretty chaotic."

"Well, the bra lady didn't seem disturbed, and I wondered why. Later Gran told me that the transsexual had the lead in a Broadway show, so all restrictions were out of the window— Mrs. Glickstein's father had been a leading actor in the Yiddish theater."

So what did the bra story have to do with losing her virginity?

"So you left the store and . . ."

Mom looked tortured. "I left the store with several Maidenform bras, a girdle, and a charge account for future needs. Luckily, Gran had a performance, so she went to the theater. I ran to the F train and headed straight for the Waldorf Luncheonette, where my pals hung out because it was right across the street from the Waldorf-Astoria Hotel and our high school. Immediately I ordered a black-and-white ice cream soda and said to pesky Georgie McGuire—he was a junior at Notre Dame, but he hung out with us because he was a silly nerd—I said, 'Georgie, you're always asking me to go for a ride. Well, today I'll say yes.'

"So we got into his dad's Chrysler and drove up to the bridge area. And that's where I became a woman."

My mother announced this with such great aplomb I didn't know what to say. So I went stupid. "But *why* did you do it?"

Her expression moved from wounded perplexity to a kind of rage. "Because I was determined not to be packaged and sold to the highest bidder like a harem girl. My future was going to be different. I was going to be a free spirit. No man would ever own me."

I blinked. "But what did freedom have to do with losing your virginity under a bridge?"

Her voice turned sarcastic. "Think about it, Lizzie. Doing it with a silly nerd the first time meant I didn't have to worry.

I didn't love Georgie. I wasn't going to have an orgasm—not yet, at least. And I couldn't care less whether he came or not. So it was simply research. You know what I mean. You try a procedure and look at the results."

"And they were?"

"I told Georgie to take me home. On the ride back, he begged and begged me to see him again, and I told him 'No way.' That's when I discovered the power women have over men. Gran had always hinted about this, but I never understood it till then."

I still didn't. "Explain, please?"

Mom looked annoyed. "Oh, for heaven's sake. You know what it's all about. All you New Girls do. You're born with choices that took me years and years of struggle. But I got them!"

She sounded proud and went back to her treasured carryall. Out came a black minidress with gauzy layers of lace and chiffon—it had shoulders and bodice and length.

Gorgeous.

"Do you think I can wear this?"

"Are you going formal?"

Mom looked nervous. "I thought I might." She paused, smiling. "Will you come with me?"

My first impulse was to refuse. That crazy bra-virginity story was so weird—it's no wonder Mom went wild after that introduction to sex.

Then I remembered the poem about me and Mom and surviving.

Lizzie, here's a perfect opportunity for you to be an adult—and be generous and supportive of your mom—even though she certainly is a bit of a flake!!!

So I lied gracefully. "Sure, Mom. It'll be a pleasure to go with you."

Chapter Fifteen

— 1 —

I WOULDN'T WISH the next few hours on any daughter. I sat next to Mom amidst a select group of film folk and watched her bouncing around au naturel with her pals in the kind of Woodstock-type festival where people got stoned and stupid in the cause of sexual freedom.

Nasty business.

I wondered about the releasing studio. Chocolate Heart had been making inexpensive films and drawing audiences. Last year three of their films earned impressive profits. My theory was this studio concentrated on small stories which were well-written so the screenplays attracted big names.

Morris Trumbull, the studio head, had worked for Sam Shapiro and learned all his tricks. Never pay too much was a golden rule. Another was, get good writers. I secretly hoped that one day I would show my very own screenplay to Trumbull, and he would say, "Excellent—we'll do it!!"

Ahem.

I wondered what Trumbull was planning for Mom's film. Each film has to have a niche, a preferred market. But *The Festival* was boring, boring, boring. Who the hell wanted to see a bunch of naked hippies running around with paint on their faces and bodies? Not me.

When the damned thing ended, we walked up the aisle of the theater. I noticed Maxim Lester leering in our direction and gave him the finger. Immediately he gave it back.

Mom asked, "So what do you think?"

"I liked it," I lied. "But no one is going to ask me to review my mother's film. Let's wait and see what people say at the party."

She smiled. I was happy to see that I had performed my daughterly duty well.

$$- 2 -$$

IN THE EARLY A.M. HOURS, the Meat Market used to be a place where butchers with bloodstained white coats stood alongside transvestite hookers at the coffee stand—both needing caffeine after a night's work. Now it was the trendiest area in Gotham. Alongside meatpacking businesses rose elegant floor-to-ceiling boutique window displays, formal French restaurants, expensive cafes and bars, and luxury residential towers where rents had skyrocketed.

Still, some of the original underground clubs hung on, where the midnight clientele worked out their fantasies. New visitors knew about the area because of the *Sex and the City* location shots.

It was no surprise that Morris Trumbull, who envied the show's success, had engaged *Le Provence* for the film party. At the entrance, two huge security guards checked our invitations. Like most guardians of the night, they wore black and lots of shiny gold jewelry. This style clashed with the current mode of dress, where everyone looked practically naked.

Inside *Le Provence* were naked backs, thighs, legs, breasts, shoulders, and midriffs. Curiously, while body parts were uncovered, girls wore turbans, Juliet caps, and large bows in their coifs, with veils extending over the face. Guess it was an attempt to be mysterious, now that everything else was on public display.

Lots of journalists were trying to be media stars. Gals wore sensual silk suits, guys open silk shirts and tailored slacks. All had the pinched look of torturous chic, the messy hair style.

The cuisine was abundant and extravagant. Centerpieces of beef filets with various sauces. A chunky olive pate alongside mahi-mahi. The usual giant prawns. Terrines of tomatoes, broccoli, zucchini, and foie gras. The dessert table was off track; only three choices, crème brûlée, chocolate mousse cake, and strawberry sorbet for people on a diet.

There was an antique soda fountain in one corner, so I pushed through the crowd of actors, publicists, family, friends, and types I couldn't identify. A towering man was in charge of the shoppe's specialty: egg creams.

"Could I have a low-fat egg cream?" a petite model next to me asked.

"No such thing." He raised his thick thumb to point at a plaque stating that only Fox's U-bet chocolate syrup was used. "It's a sin even to think that way."

"Could I have one very cold egg cream?" I ordered confidently.

He smiled at me, his red cheeks glowing. He poured two fingers of milk into a glass, then pumped lots and lots of syrup. He stirred the concoction together, adding seltzer from a high-pressure soda head. As the snowy white foam rose in the glass, my lips grew taut.

This experienced soda man knew a fan when he saw one. "Taste it—see if it's good," he said.

I did. And I was in heaven.

— 3 —

UNFORTUNATELY, I DIDN'T STAY there long. As I turned, I spotted Ronald Eldridge signaling me to join him. I looked around for Mom, whom I'd lost in my rush for caloric intake, and saw her in a corner surrounded by paparazzi. Ouch! This meant that Morris Trumbull was planning to make *The Festival* a mainstream hit.

Damn! I thought Mom's cinema dalliance could remain discreet. An art theater release. The university circuit. Silly of me. Trumbull was giving this type of party to start a scandal.

Okay. Later for Trumbull. Now I had to prepare myself for a talk with my former employer. So I stopped at the bar and ordered a martini. I gulped it down, then ordered another, slowly becoming aware of a sad fact: chocolate egg creams and martinis don't mingle well. The combination left me feeling slightly woozy.

I looked around for the loo, but it was too late. Ron was at my side. "So where the hell have you been? I've been phoning you."

"I've been around."

"Look, I got a great idea. I want you to do a feature on your mother. It'll be great. Intellectual author and university professor caught with her bloomers down."

"No way."

"I'll put you on staff. You always wanted that, didn't you? You'll be one of us."

"Is this Harry's idea?"

He glowered. "Nope. Harry's a gentleman. He's almost British."

"Yeah. Right. And he's shagging your girlfriend."

Whoops! Where did that come from?

Ron turned chalk-white and checked to see if anyone had heard my stupid revelation. "Don't be vulgar," he said. "I'm a happily married man and don't have girlfriends. Besides, Harry is a bachelor. He can date any woman he wishes to see. By the way isn't he doing you, too?"

I grabbed a glass from a tray of pink drinks that just went by. Slurp. Slurp. I was ready for anything more he had to say.

Or so I thought.

"Lizzie, you've a good head on your shoulders. You know all about films, and actors, and production costs, and all the gossip. You have values about films which I respect." He stared right through me. "But you have a hard heart and a dry CUNT and that's going to be the death of your career."

I wanted to shout I was not dry in the C. but decided not to. Instead, my mouth seemed to take off on its own.

"And what about Sherry's C . . . ? She's doing you, and Harry, and whoever else comes along."

"I don't know what you're talking about," Ron said. Someone tapped the publisher on the shoulder, but he went on.

"My offer is still on the table. We can do an exclusive. Big headlines in the entertainment section. Wouldn't you like that?"

"*I don't think so!!*"

I threw my drink at him.

"Why did you do that?" Harry said, suddenly beside me.

"She's a loose cannon!" Ron growled at Harry, his dripping face stony. "I don't know why you still want her around."

Then he disappeared into the crowd.

– 4 –

"YEAH, I'M A LOOSE CANNON." I stumbled badly, and Harry caught me. "I'm a b-a-a-d girl. With a b-a-a-d mom."

"Well, I see where you get your craziness. Lizzie, you have to stop screwing around," he sermonized. "You need someone to love you."

I felt like vomiting, but the loyal words still came. "My mother loved my dad, and then she was alone. No one helped her."

"But you don't need to do it alone. I'm here."

"Right. Sure. Didn't you just fire me?"

"Did that."

"Why? And don't ask me to believe you don't like my work!"

"That wasn't the reason."

"Was it because Sherry wanted more of your time and leaned on Ron?"

"Not so."

"Then why?"

"Because I have plans . . ."

– 5 –

WHATEVER ELSE HE WAS going to say got lost as the lights dimmed, a screen descended against one wall, and acid rock bellowed from speakers. Then clips of Mom's nude ass appeared, seeming to dance to the music. The audience uttered a chorus of tacky comments—in this crowd, these were meant as compliments.

"This is sick!!" I broke free from Harry and stormed my way into the crowd around Trumbull.

"You *bastard*," I shouted.

Damn him! He looked so innocent, I had to mess him up. So I clenched my fist and hit him square in the nose. Blood splurted, but it wasn't enough for me.

So I kicked him hard in the groin.

And as he fell to the ground, I realized this incredibly theatrical—and illegal—incident was being immortalized by the *veree* observant paparazzi.

Chapter Sixteen

— 1 —

"I'M SICK OF MY LIFE," I told my best buddies, Tony and Fancy, the next morning whilst drinking a cappuccino in *The Record*'s bisexual toilet. (Ron labeled the place after seeing too many episodes of *Ally McBeal*, another of his obsessions.)

"Oh, Lizzie! Don't carry on so. It isn't as bad as you think," Tony, my best male buddy turned swain, made dismissive gestures.

"You're unstoppable. Hugely charismatic," Fancy said without a jesting tone in her voice—admirable, under the dire circumstances.

"And you have an incredible knack of making everybody you meet feel special," Tony agreed, though he sounded a bit facetious.

"Tell me, though," I asked *tres* seriously, "why is it that single women are always burned by the media spotlight? Every daily paper carries a story about so-and-so being a binge drinker. The evening news will talk about her being a sexual predator. Broadcast newsmags will reveal that she took some pills when she was fifteen years old. The men in these stories never get mentioned, though they might be sleeping around, drinking anything that's handy, and probably have ruined more lives—if not personally, then certainly in business. SO WHY ARE ONLY SINGLE WOMEN DRIVEN THROUGH THESE CONSTANT MEDIA INQUISITIONS??"

Fancy looked at Tony, and they both shook their heads, conveying that this was a serious situation.

It was.

I delivered my diatribe whilst sitting up on a sink top banging my New Balance running shoes against the base as water thundered from the faucet onto *The Morning Press*— one of *The Record's* competitors which supposedly covered world events, Washington politics and media goings-on in equal importance. But in a spot usually reserved for events like winning a pennant or an Oscar, today the headline was TOUGH CRITIC. It appeared over a large blowup of my dalliance (if you can call it that) with Morris Trumbull.

The caption read:

> Elizabeth Parsons, film critic for *The Record,* whacks Chocolate Heart Films Prez Morris Trumbull at the premiere party for *The Festival,* a Sixties documentary which features Ms. Parsons' mom, author and professor Margaret Parsons, in the nude. We can only assume that Lizzie, who has often campaigned for honesty in film, doesn't approve of full disclosure if her mom's involved.

"This is going to create a controversy which will generate an audience for that stupid film among perverts, sexologists, and curiosity seekers. There'll be lots of publicity, reviews, interviews, and all that jazz."

"Don't be a hypocrite, Lizzie," Fancy said. "This is what we work at."

"I know." The words seemed to stick in my throat. "I know."

Feeling totally responsible for the state of the media in this country and throughout the globe, I rambled on. "You know what happens if this kind of paparazzi photo goes big. It'll appear on all the entertainment and so-called TV news reports. They'll broadcast Mom's ass to damage her very impressive authorship and alienate her professional colleagues. I can just see the headlines now."

I cringed at this reality. "They'll stab, stab, stab. There are absolutely NO KIND WORDS in media reporting. I ought to know! I write this stuff!"

"Lizzie, that's what the media game is all about. I don't see why you're fussing about it. You're acting like a civilian—a normal girl," Tony said pointedly.

"But I am a girl!"

"You're not," Fancy said. "Remember our mantra."

"Well, I *feel* like a girl," I wailed.

Tears fell on my flushed cheeks. Dear Fancy produced tissues from her purse and gingerly dabbed at my eyes. "You are a girl," she whispered. "But you're also a JANO-ite. Don't ever forget that."

Totally unlike a JANO-ite, I whimpered with self-pity. "Thanks for trying to make me sane, but I've had a *veree* difficult night—watching too many films, eating chocolate eclair ice cream, and not answering Harry's calls."

"Why didn't you talk to Harry?" Tony queried.

"Because I feel awful and ashamed. I don't know what he wants from me, and I don't know what I want from him, either. Harry is the perfect man—straight, single, with no responsibilities, and a healthy bank balance. He's a man who loves what I love: good reporting, interesting films, and now I've discovered he also loves interior decorating."

Fancy rolled her eyes insinuatingly.

"No, it's all woodsy stuff," I quickly interjected. "No froufrou at all."

"So he's not gay? Why is it that every single man in Manhattan is suspected of being gay and has to go through this inquisition?" Tony said angrily.

Swiftly, Fancy responded. "Because the number of uncertain men has doubled over the past two decades. In fact, I fear that there will be a million bachelors soon who'll be running scared of New Women."

"In other words, you hope some of these bachelors are gay!!" Tony summarized.

"Absolutely," I said. "Because if that weren't so, we JANO-ites would dump the entire love situation and become nuns. Wouldn't we, Fancy?"

"I wouldn't go that far, but it certainly would be quite a competition for the few men with large penises, open hearts, interesting minds, and heterosexual interests," my erstwhile colleague agreed.

"Besides, my Darling Lad is to die for. His boyish good looks, his wicked sense of humor—I want to take him home and SMOTHER him. That's what I *really* want." I broke out in a sweat. "Harry simply doesn't rate next to my sweetie."

They moaned in unison.

"First of all, he isn't *yours*. Let's have some reality here." Tony spoke the truth cruelly. "And secondly, Harry looks as much like the Brit as anyone can."

He turned to Fancy, who nodded. "That's why we assumed he was a good match for you. Harry is not only living in the real world of flesh and blood and orgasms, but when you look at him in bed, with his tousled hair and his charming smile, you can imagine that he is INDEED your Lad."

"That wouldn't be fair to Harry," I protested.

"Who wants to be fair?" they asked in unison.

I answered. "A good question, and one that should be interwoven in our cause of men and women and the state of sex in this year of our life, along with issues like terrorism, and the wars which keep cropping up all over the globe, and the fact that the international cinema scene is one big global mess, as well."

Tony countered. "Not to mention the fact that because most Gotham girls go to the gym, they have no bottoms and no breasts."

He sighed. "So men like me go to diners on Tenth Avenue to meet Spanish waitresses who do have those physical endowments necessary for the behavior known as sexual excitement—leading to bed-process."

Tony said all this whilst sneaking a smoke, though there was a huge NO SMOKING sign on the wall.

Distracted, Fancy asked Tony, "When did you begin smoking?"

"As soon as the city passed the no-smoking law."

Her brow wrinkled. "And why is that?"

"Because it's a new way to meet women. Look, I'm tired of schmoozing it up at bars and dancing my tail off in trendy clubs. Now, all I have to do is walk down the street, stop at the place of my choice, and in front of it will be two or three slender pretties, smoking away. Ordinarily, they probably wouldn't speak to me. But once I light up—well— it's magic! They begin to identify with me, so it's much easier to make out.

"It's even cheaper. You don't have to buy her a drink. It goes this way. I ask her for a light, trying to be cool, and then we talk about how we hate nonsmokers and after a ciggie or two, I get a cab and take her home. It's awesome!"

"Does she ever go to your place?" A good media person, Fancy slipped into interview mode, quick to be on the cutting edge of this new phenomenon.

"I have to be careful about that. Last time I took a girl home, she went into my bathroom and started giggling when she saw my exfoliating gycolic acid. Said she didn't know that men did that, too."

"Did you score?"

He shook his head. "She walked out. When I asked her why, she said 'I can support myself, but I would like a man in my life. What I don't need is a man who has the same equipment in the bathroom as I have. That'll make me wonder just who I am and what I'm supposed to do with him sexually.'"

– 2 –

"Ah, SEX, SEX, SEX. The ONLY important issue in our lives." I was *veree* sarcastic with Tony. "I have a really awful scandal going on here, and you're going on about how to meet girls. Grow up."

"Oh, can it, Lizzie. Don't point a finger at a fellow addict. You could talk about your Brit and Harry f-o-r-e-v-e-r."

"It's a serious matter." I tried to defend myself.

"So is my sex life. Look, I took to my bed for two days without eating anything after that bitch walked out laughing. I was devastated. I called my shrink and said, 'Are you sure this spa stuff is manly?' We've talked about it, you know, and he said, 'Tony. Do you like the way the stuff feels?' and I said, 'Yes,' and he said, 'then use it and enjoy it. And don't let anyone tell you there's anything wrong with rubbing down your skin.'"

Tony made a strange face, *veree* hostile. "So don't be a bitch! You have everything a girl could want. You're gorgeous. You have Harry crazy over you. Honey, just be more focused and less neurotic, and you'll come out of all of this okay."

"How divine was that?" I demanded ungratefully.

"Hey, I've got an idea. Why don't you just start over as a virgin!" he shot back.

Shit!

With that, I took the soggy remainder of *The Morning Press*, tore it up in minuscule pieces, jumped down from the sink, and pushed the papier-mâché mess into one of the toilet bowls.

"Don't flush," Fancy warned.

But I did.

The toilet backed up and water seeped across the elegant lavender tiles that Ron had imported from Mexico because Frida Kahlo had lived there. (Another of his obsessions.)

When the messy flood threatened the sink area, I squirmed. But Fancy laughed, a *veree* satisfying, rich sound. Then she leaned over to me and gave me the thumbs-up as we retreated to the other side of the room where the makeup tables were.

Tony was annoyed. "Oh, you never listen," he complained.

Fancy spoke up. "That's our dear Lizzie's metier. She's stylish and chatty and representative of everything in films today."

— 3 —

WHAT DOES A FILM CRITIC do when confronted by serious life events? This was clearly my question of the moment.

Answer . . . I didn't know.

– 4 –

SOMETIMES I THINK THAT other people have a secret place where they hide all their generosity. Why else would most people tend to be niggardly and selfish? In my more compassionate moments I knew it was because people felt dissatisfied with their lives. Their dreams have never been realized, and they become despairing and sad—and sometimes, nasty.

They give up.

"Never give up," my Gran taught me.

So why had I given up on Harry? A few nights ago, we told each other sweet lies. Afterwards, his dark-blue eyes focused on me as if I were the only person worth looking at in this wicked world. When he caressed my cheek, I noticed that his hand was trembling. His lips touched mine, his tongue lingering. I felt giddy, silly, stupid . . .

Then I felt scared.

Be careful, my heart said to me, *don't get too comfortable— this could all disappear in a moment.*

– 5 –

MAYBE THAT'S WHAT WAS WRONG with my life. I didn't trust anyone. It was Mom's fault. She'd raised me to be an independent, confident girl who didn't need help. A flesh-and-blood archetype who would affect future generations of women. What my Gran would call "a *no-nonsense jane.*"

A *jane* who could reach both the left and right wings, because she was so true to her convictions. A darling of critics and producers alike. The kind of *jane* who is on every list which celebrates the female sex.

A *jane* who can dictate the pace and power of her love life. A *jane* who is unwilling to compromise and is very intolerant of men who are crap. A *jane* who enjoys the single life and doesn't mind cleaning her apartment whilst speaking to her power colleagues on the cell phone about corporate policies.

A *jane* who shares female camaraderie and strives for greater and grander things for all members of her gender. A *jane* who views herself as an inspiration to any man. A *jane* who doesn't have to drink, smoke, take drugs, and have sex to be lovable.

In fact, a *jane* who was very much like dear Gran.

But what did Gran do in a real crisis?

And what did Jane Austen do?

I knew Elizabeth Bennet simply carried on with her life— arranging flowers, reading books, having tea, taking long walks. But how was she feeling deep inside? I simply didn't know.

Then it occurred to me that there was one person who might.

Edgar Meredith, Guardian of Jane Austen's Holiness, Adviser to Screenwriters, Mentor, Man-About-Town, Professor, and the man who kept his personal life mysterious to all.

— 6 —

WE WERE SITTING IN AN OUTDOOR café where beautiful, tall blonde women pushed baby carriages ferrying beautiful blonde babies, and men and women of all colors, sizes, and shapes walked dogs of all colors, sizes, and shapes, and an unusual number of men strolled by holding hands.

When I asked Edgar what he thought of my difficulties with love, sex, men, a mother's nudity, and life in general, he said, "Don't look at me for any answers, Lizzie."

But in the way he said it, strangely enough, I recognized that Edgar Meredith had indeed been in love—and had lost.

"Tell me about her . . . him?"

At first, Edgar looked stunned, as if I'd zapped him right in the noggin. But then his expression turned churlish, as if reliving this memory would cause him embarrassment.

"Please . . ." I pleaded in my best *sweet-jane* manner. (Yes, I admit I use the girl thing when necessary.)

"Okay. I'll answer your question. But swear on your mother you'll never repeat any of it."

"I swear," I promised.

Edgar spoke in a low voice. "I lost my heart in 1977. I was coming home from a film screening and walked by the Greenwich Street Bar. The doors were open, Elvis Presley's voice was blaring out. I went in, and on the blackboard someone had scrawled, *Elvis is dead.* That's when I met the love of my life, Pauline Raichur."

"*The* Pauline Raichur?"

He nodded. "Yes, the infamous actress, may she rest in peace." He paused, then, "She wore a white cotton dress and white carnations in her jet-black hair. She was heavily rouged, so I knew she was in show business. I sat at the bar and put my briefcase down, so she immediately knew I was media—we all used the same battered leather cases back then. She came up to me and whispered in my ear, 'I regret that I will never fuck Elvis.' And I was hers.

"That year I experimented with pills, liquor, and my

174 ⚞ SEX & SENSIBILITY

aphrodisiac sleep-over lover. My only interest in life was how long it would be between saying goodbye to Pauline—and hello again. I was possessed. I lost all my bearings and almost lost my job. Without her next to me, I was unmanageable.

"Then one day, she said to me, 'I don't love you anymore.'"

I was overwhelmed with sadness. Edgar was always so daunting in his passion for life, for Jane Austen, and films. It was a shock to see him rejected, even in memory.

"What happened?"

"I began to teach film. And I turned gay . . . or maybe I should say, I returned to being gay."

"Did that help?"

"A bit. Look, I'm an eccentric, Cambridge-educated film studies professor, a bit of a celebrity. I can get tables in restaurants even though I'm often rumpled and unshaven."

Edgar pushed back his anarchic gray hair and straightened the spectacles that made him look like Hercule Poirot. "In gay circles I'm terribly popular, because whenever I have two martinis my British accent returns, and I am absolutely charming." He laughed, but with a cruel twist. "To most of my pals, I'm witty and droll."

"But hasn't anyone else . . ."

He shook his head. "You can't move on until you've completely healed from pain. I haven't yet. Neither have you, Lizzie."

I was taken aback as he continued. "That's why you're so hung up on this man-woman thing. You and your buddies talk and talk about *relationships* as if they exist in a vacuum, as if you can fit love in between shopping for Manolos, bitching about work, and watching films.

"But that's not so. True love is rare and only rushes into a person's life one time—sometimes twice. The rest of the time is all about sex for fun and emotional profit. So . . ." he peered down at me from his guru perch . . ."You've simply got to decide about Harry. Are you willing to die for him?"

"That's pretty rash."

"Not with your past. Remember, your father abandoned you and Maggie. That's got to mean something serious down deep in the place where your heart suffers."

I insisted, "But that's all in the past."

"Not so. Your past can spoil your future, Lizzie, if someone has captured your heart and refuses to let go."

"Like my Darling Lad has??" He nodded. "But why haven't you spoken of this at JANO?"

"Lizzie," he sounded impatient with me. "I'm a man. *Men don't weep in public.*"

Chapter Seventeen

— 1 —

BUT *MEN* SURE WERE GOOD at denouncements, especially on television. I choked on my coffee the next morning listening to Jeffrey Walton, a fundamentalist spokesperson, call my mother "an unfortunate lady—a symbol of decadence who should not be allowed in our educational system."

Walton's Southern accent was unbearably hideous, the kind that an actress might use in a Tennessee Williams play out of a special theatrical masochism.

Walton certainly enjoyed important contacts—what followed was a media blitz plugging his outfit, inappropriately named "People for America." My predictions had come true. TV news bites featured Mom's nudity plus Walton's claims that she was unfit to teach. But the coverage didn't include me (which I was happy about). Still, it was puzzling.

At teatime I learned why. I'd had two cuppas when Ron phoned and explained.

(Yes, once again I was sipping tea and smoothing U.S. jam on tiny biscuits packed in a lovely tin from the U.K. The biscuits were appropriately named Mint Smoothers.)

Ron's voice sounded too pleasant, so I knew he wanted something from me. "Lizzie, I'm giving you a chance to redeem your mother."

"My mother doesn't need redemption."

"Don't be that way. I'm doing you a real favor."

"Talk to me, Ron."

"There's too much buzz about *The Festival,* so it's totally urgent that we publish a serious review. Since you're on record defending the freedom of art in films, you should do it."

I objected. "I can't review a film featuring my mother." I paused and stuffed two smoothers into my mouth at the same time. "C-a-a-n I?" I mumbled.

"What the hell is wrong with you? Do you have your mouth wrapped around—uh, is Harry there?"

"Noooooo."

He chuckled in disbelief. "Okay, if he's there, say hello as soon as your mouth is free."

I almost slammed the phone down, but concern for Mom kept me sane. "Go on," I said.

"Lizzie, here's your opportunity to screw these stupid bastards who are hogging television time that belongs to serious film criticism."

About that, he was making sense. "Ron, I don't understand. Why have I been spared the rotten limelight on this story?" I asked.

He answered gleefully. "That's Harry's doing. You should give him another kiss."

"Harry's not here. What do you mean, it's his doing?"

"You know how well-respected Harry is. When he asked his peers to keep you out of the story, most of them agreed. Besides asking for personal favors, Harry made the case that no media person would do well in the spotlight."

"Too true."

"So you owe him."

"Uh-huh."

"Are you sure he's not there?"

"Give it up, Ron."

Ron's voice turned authoritarian, which meant he was about to hustle me. "You also owe your mom! Defend the film, defend her right to bare her ass! Be the person you really are! Be the strong advocate for film ethics, non-censorship, and media rights that we've championed you as!" He took a deep breath and added, *"Be a media narcissist!"*

After the way he fired me, I probably should tell Ron to shove his media narcissist nonsense. But I have unique survival skills, partly inherited and partly learned in the competitive media workplace.

To wit: I've indisputably become an operator, a hustler, a manipulator like ALL media people. In two seconds, I can generally run a scam to get a story or a quote. Yes, I've learned my lessons working for the Media Mafia.

Genetically, I cling to Grandmother Alice's advice: "Always have something in the vault." If my media career tanked, I'd become a screenwriter, pawn one of Alice's diamond brooches, and live on coffee and toast for a year.

(But the thought of living in a garret like those French writers did whilst writing their explosive, sensual novels made me retch.)

Ron's demands brought me back to reality. "Are you there?"

I immediately poured another cuppa. "I'll think about it."

"Don't think . . . do. That's the rule I learned a long time ago. It's one I live by."

"So you're divorcing Mrs. Eldridge?"

"You betcha."

— 2 —

WHEN I READ AN AFTERNOON paper, I found an article
ridiculing Mom, Gran, and moi.

This guy was smooth. Bigelow Barnett first listed Mom's
impressive professional works and went on to say that Alice
Parsons was a living legend among theater gypsies (dancers).
Then he commented that both were "that kind of women" and
added, so was Lizzie Parsons, granddaughter of the fab Alice
and daughter of the infamous Maggie. Didn't she work for
The Village Record? And hadn't she defended sinful films like
American Beauty?

(To tell you the truth, I don't know why this film about
infidelity upset so many religiosos. My guess it was all about
the rose blanket on that pretty young thing.)

Immediately I phoned Bigelow Barnett and ranted off a
list of curses I don't want to repeat, lest I offend.

"Lizzie, sweetie," he said, pretending to be a pal.

For the record, we weren't friends. I'd met him once after
tripping and falling under a table at a grand soiree, to find the
space inhabited by BB and CD, whom I will not identify
because they will sue me big time.

I corrected him. "Bigelow, we don't know each other."

He dodged like a good reporter. "I'm on your side. In fact,
I've done you a great big fave."

"And what is that?"

"I didn't mention your dad."

My body turned cold. "What does that mean?"

"Then you don't know?"

My fear turned into paralysis. I could hardly hold the

phone to my ear, so I put it on the speaker in anticipation of the dead faint that was coming. "Know what?"

"According to my sources, your dad has pulled a Salinger."

"Huh?"

"He left your mom and his career as a film producer for Sam Shapiro to disappear into the desert, where nobody knows what he's doing—or where he's living."

Oh-oh. Here it comes.

"So if this story gets any bigger," Bigelow boasted, "I'm going to have to go West and poke around—see if I can find Mr. Nick Blakely. Maybe he's one of those wandering types who roam the desert quoting Scriptures to three wives and twelve children. Imagine, Lizzie! You could have a whole family out there that you know nothing about."

"Or maybe he's one of those strange guys who kidnap young girls. If you're very lucky, he might be a serial killer. Hey, Bigelow! Wouldn't that be great for your headlines?"

"Lizzie, you're losing it."

Yes, I was. I'd spent too many years wondering where Dad was, deciding that if he married again, I wouldn't want to know. The reason was that it would be too hurtful for my mother. She'd had enough pain in her life.

I kept my mind on track and tried to be clever. "Bigelow? Is this story really worth your time and effort?"

"Sure thing. Our readers love stories about fallen women. And a *family of fallen women* should earn BIG numbers."

− 3 −

SURE, MOM DIDN'T FOLLOW the rules—but she tried to be a good mother. All the anger, heartbreak, broken dreams, and lost hopes she must have felt never daunted her enthusiasm for our lives. Of course, like any kid, I wanted my mother to be like other mothers. Only Mom wasn't. And I didn't have any pro-totype to emulate, because when I was growing up, single mothers were hard to find in films or on TV. Years later, when I studied film at college, I realized that in early films, single women were sinners who had to pay dearly—for instance, Barbara Stanwyck in *Stella Dallas*, a classic 1937 film. In this film Babs is a victim, but I liked her better as a hard-boiled girl of easy virtue in 1933's *Baby Face* or the double-crossing blonde wife in 1944's *Double Indemnity*.

(I know, I know, this is *veree* revealing of my character.)

I also adored Joan Crawford in *Mildred Pierce*, which won her an Oscar. With her padded shoulders, flounced dresses, and high-heeled anklets, she often played a single woman harassed by a man. And sometimes she shot him.

These films, produced before I was born, only offered rotten, raw lives for women who didn't follow the rules.

Has anything really changed?

Because of my personal bias, I've always been *veree* careful when reviewing films about mothers who are sinners or vanishing dads. I try to keep a professional focus always, knowing that if I give in to my feelings, memories will come back and destroy me.

But I worried that my inability to *suffer* for sins commit-ted in the name of love might affect my critiques.

Several years ago a French director accused me of "only skimming the surface" of his film. In it, a woman was pun-ished severely (having her head severed) because she was unfaithful—not to her husband, but to her lover!

Quite unprofessionally, I told him he was a typical French misogynistic bastard.

He replied that I was an American media whore.

He may be correct, though most of the time I hate what the media is capable of. Since most scandals happen to other people, I never get too involved. I've rationalized that the media was only as bad as its readers, and that readers got bored with "good" stories.

But this story is different. It's my mother who's the target of all this slime. If Bigelow gets lucky and prints Dad's whereabouts—and if Dad is happily married with lots of babies—that'll really break Mom.

But the truth is, I miss Dad. I want to ask him, "Why did you leave us? Was it my fault? Can you forgive me, and will you come back if I promise to be a *good girl?*"

– 4 –

THAT AFTERNOON, I E-MAILED Fancy that I was sending *The Festival* review. But what could I say about a film I hated?

Hey, Lizzie, I told myself, *you don't write this one from your brain . . .*

You write it from your heart.

So I began:

```
The Festival, a retro look at the Sixties
culture, offers the type of On The Road
footage that was very popular in films of
that era. The actors are very animated and
spontaneous, conveying a childlike inno-
cence throughout this outdoor romp.
     Among them is a woman who was part of
those rebellious times when sex and drugs
```

and public nudity were part of the Sexual
and Political Revolutions. Shimmying her
bare buttocks along with her playmates
during this Sixties love-in was her generation's way of fighting the conser-
vatism and censorship of that era.

This woman is my mother, Maggie Parsons.

In the Sixties, she was a flower child.
Today she is a published author and university professor. A feminist icon, her
readers and students adore her—she is a
force to be reckoned with.

My mother makes no apologies for her
behavior in this film. Instead, she
views this experience as being typical-
ly American. We are lucky to live in a
country where freedoms are guaranteed by
the Constitution.

As for me, I'm proud of my mom.

$$- 5 -$$

AFTER I FAXED THE PAGES to Fancy, I wept. I had finally
done something generous for Mom. *Silly goose*, I told myself.
But somehow this whole experience made me feel melancholy. It brought back an entire past I wanted to avoid.

Too, I was nervous about how it would be received. I had
always worked hard to be objective, pooh-poohing other journalists who wrote of personal experiences. So I could see my

competitors laughing outright. They'd say, "Oh, Lizzie Parsons
has finally cracked."

But I didn't care, because I knew Mom would love the
piece.

Now I needed support, someone to hold me, someone to
cherish me.

I remembered Gran's advice: "Whenever you want
something from someone, always bring a gift first."

So I rushed out and bought an expensive silk scarf at
Barney's, the kind that my Darling Lad always wore. And as I
rounded the corner to Commerce Street, I stopped at a florist
and bought two dozen red roses.

American Beauty, I thought, you can work for me, too.

– 6 –

WHEN HARRY ANSWERED the door, he was in BVDs with
red hearts on the borders and looked *tres* adorable.

"Well, look who's here," he said. He was holding a fax,
which he waved about. "They just sent me your piece. It's
wonderful, Lizzie. I'm proud of you."

"Are you going to edit it?"

"No way. It's perfect."

A writer's fantasy. I rushed him, and we toppled onto the
floor. I kissed him, landing smooches on every part of his
nakedness and then some. It took a while to give him all the
gifts I had for him.

Afterwards, Harry bemoaned the fact that the petals from
two dozen roses simply couldn't cover us. "I wonder how
many roses they used in the film—do you know, Lizzie?"

"Sorry. But I'll find out," I promised.

When Harry opened the Barney's box, he smiled. "A Brit lad scarf," he said mischievously. I laughed, wrapped it around his chest, and kissed both his nipples. Harry smiled happily. "What's all this for, Lizzie?"

"It's for being a wonderful man. Thank you for using your contacts to keep me out of this stupid scandal."

"And . . . ?"

I looked into his deep-blue eyes. Funny thing, I'd never noticed that Harry had that primitive masculine energy I loved. That was probably because most of our relationship was played out in our respective roles of media critic and editor, which was totally intellectual—or tried to be.

But now I could see that he had that wonderful raw energy of a rock star.

Girlfriends! You know what I'm talking about!

Wow! What a manly creature! True, he doesn't have my Darling Lad's wonderfully risque sense of humor. *I have to admit that is my favorite turn-on!!* However, Harry transformed his male energy into something very noble.

Hadn't he tried to rescue me?

Veree admirable.

"And . . . ?" he repeated, waiting.

"I don't want it too hard." I flustered as he nodded. "I mean what's between us." His eyebrows raised, and he totally laughed. "No, I mean our relationship, Harry." I blushed. "Please don't make fun of me. I'm trying to say something really difficult."

Tenderly, he kissed the edge of my nose on the scar from my skating accident. "Okay, then," he whispered, "I'll be good."

"I'll try to keep it all sane and sensible."

"My sweet darling," Harry said, "I don't love you because you're sane and sensible. I love you because you're a real girl

186 9~~ SEX & SENSIBILITY

under that sophisticated, genius-brainchild cloak you're so fond of wearing. But I don't want you to change one thing."

"Really, Harry?"

"Yes, really. I love you for exactly who you are."

I gasped. "You mean like Mark Darcy loves Bridget Jones?"

"Uh-huh."

He kissed me soundly. I enjoyed it, I must say. But all the while, I thought—hey, it was Daniel Cleaver (not Mark Darcy) whom I loved in *Bridget Jones' Diary* . . . the bad sod who cheated on her while they were having GREAT sex.

I was soooo confused.

Shouldn't great sex lead to GREAT love?

Hmmmmm!

Jane Austen thought great love led to GREAT sex.

Oh fuck!
And Double Fuck!

Chapter Eighteen

— 1 —

"LIZZIE, BABY, things have exploded," Morris Trumbull's voice crackled over the phone.

He'd called and asked me to drop in at his office down in Chinatown. "Pronto," he said. "I'll send a car. What would you like for lunch?"

"Dumplings," I answered, without hesitation.

I arrived to find four different types of dumplings on trays. I tasted several while listening to Trumbull's pitch.

Wiping his mouth with his handkerchief—he ate dumplings even faster than moi—he turned to his assistant, Felicia Ramos. "Maggie's story is a hot property. Right, hon?"

"She'll be toast if we don't capitalize on it NOW," the petite girl announced.

She was small but didn't seem to have any problem about that. Her skin was olive, which softened her harsh green eyes. Long black hair was pulled into a topknot that looked like some kind of explosion. She was batting a tennis racket at various plants in the office whilst wearing a brilliant smile.

"It's going to be a goddam circus out there, with everybody just dipping in and writing whatever the hell they think is going to do it," she said forthrightly.

I had the feeling this girlfriend had a pretty strong, up-front, confrontational attitude. Looking at the poor plants, though, I thought she should take some anger-management workshops.

Trumbull took the mike . . . so to speak. "If you don't write the screenplay, someone else will!"

"I'm not sure I want to do that. It's my mother we're talking about, not some ninny celebrity."

"Hey," Felicia cooed. "Mama is BIG news. Every gossip column is featuring her story. It's got everything—romance and scandal, two things you can't top."

She took a second to swat at a geranium. I swear I heard the plant moan with pain.

Trumbull jumped in again. "We've learned how to sell celeb gossip from the Brits, who do it so well. For every star there's a sideshow: the love affairs, the frothy photos poolside, the dates at award events, the fashions, all on those pretty page layouts on glossy paper. The audience feels guilty, but they buy those magazines and read them from cover to cover."

"That's not much to read," I quipped, but no one laughed. Instead, the two maniacs had stone-faced looks, so I got serious. "I won't have the final say on the story, and because of the nudity, there's a risk that the film will be aimed at the tits-and-ass audience."

Trumbull pontificated nicely. "Honey, we'll package it as a woman's film. Story goes like this: from a hippie, to a single mother, to a real writer, to an educator. It'll be the kind of film that encourages little girls to be the best they can be."

"Impressive," I lied. "But Mom might be totally against it."

"I don't think so," Felicia spoke in a too-nice, tippy-top tone of voice that made me dub her Twinkie. "All writers want to be film stars. They bust their asses sitting at the computer alone all day. When they break for lunch and turn on the TV, they see silly girls being photographed in fabulous homes, wearing gorgeous dresses and jewelry, about to go out on the town arm in arm with cute guys."

"Not true," I protested.

Trumbull grinned. "Heard you were a real serious fan of a certain cute Brit."

I coughed and tried to look intellectual. "Don't know who you mean."

"And you'd like to sleep with him? Right?" Impatient now, Twinkie hunted for an edge. "He's one tasty morsel."

Well, I wouldn't put it like that!

– 2 –

"WHAT KIND OF AN AUDIENCE are you aiming for?" I asked, still doing the serious intellectual shtick.

"We'll package it in a way that's upbeat. It'll have terrific historical value. The Sixties thing!" Twinkie giggled. "There's a bottomless appetite for all those stoned people."

"Mom wasn't on drugs. I want to be certain that you understand that."

"Anything you say," she said facetiously.

I began to dislike her intensely. She was a bit twisted, as if she were still rehearsing being a person, instead of actually being one. But I had to be careful, because if we got into a clash, the project (if there was a project) would turn into World War III. I'd reviewed films with that kind of history. They all sucked.

I was totally professional. "I have some qualms about it. I have to give this a lot of thought."

(Translation: I wanted to discuss this with Edgar and the JANO people, as well as Mom. But never tell stuff like that to producers, or they'll scale down your price.)

Now Twinkie looked restless. Like everybody her age (about twenty?) anything that took more than five minutes to consider was viewed as too difficult.

So she pursued the storyline. "Tell me about your Mom. Did she sleep around? Did she only sleep with guys who proposed? Or was she a hoochie?"

"Hardly." I sounded a bit pompous, and my sweet tooth suddenly kicked in. Oh, for a piece of dark chocolate—preferably from Belgium.

"Everybody lies!" Trumbull announced snidely.

Twinkie waved at him to keep quiet. "So she was a Mother T? Ooh, those babes are tough—they make their guys fall into place. It's real serious, especially if the poor bastards fall in love."

"What's a Mother T?" I wanted to hear more.

"A Mother T? She watches her guy strut his stuff and stays *sooo* calm. Oh, she might flick her tongue casually—you catch my drift?" I nodded. "And when her guy is practically falling to the floor, she smokes him. She does it sweetly, like honey. She's a real zinger, sweet and hard at the same time. This girlfriend knows how to do it. She's given it a lot of thought and practiced in front of the mirror."

I was fascinated, so I kept very quiet.

"A Mother T makes her man writhe with pain. She watches as his head spins around like a doll's while she sticks pins into him. When he comes near her for a hug, Mother gives him the foot right in the place he treasures the most—his big COCK!"

Twinkie took a deep breath and smiled. "But she's just testing him, to see if he's a REAL man."

That sounded familiar.

Twinkie coughed hoarsely and picked up a bottle of nasal spray. Two sniffs and her eyes went stoned and cold. I wondered what the hell was in that bottle.

That's when I realized that if I wrote films, this was the type of "professional" I'd be working with. Though I wasn't much older than Twinkie, I felt ancient because I spoke English.

"Lizzie—baby. Feely, here, has made a good case. What do you think?"

Feely? No way.

"I can't give you an answer right now."

Trumbull marched on. "Better decide in a hurry, babe. Sam Shapiro is thinking of mounting a production—he claims he's got the inside track, 'cause he knew your folks. Says he was there when your mom wigged out over your dad's extracurricular job actions."

I knew where this was going. "My dad isn't around to defend himself. I want him kept out of the film."

"Where the hell is he?" Trumbull demanded.

"Don't know."

Twinkie hummed suspiciously.

"You don't know?" Trumbull repeated. "You're a reporter, and don't know where your dad is?"

As he turned away, the look he directed to his assistant conveyed the idea that they'd been robbed.

"Yo, girl," the fun-loving gal said. "I suggest you get busy and look for your papa."

"I can't do that."

"Why, precisely?" Trumbull hissed.

"My mother has always kept their relationship very private, and I couldn't hurt her."

"If that's the case, if you want to protect your mom, I suggest you get on your laptop and write this story. Because if someone else does it, they'll probably screw things up."

Trumbull looked ominous. "Every family has skeletons in the closet, and yours does, too."

Did he know something? I felt frantic, so I used a delaying tactic. "I'll get back to you."

"Real quick!" Trumbull insisted.

Miss Twinkie shrugged and aimed her index finger at me. "Don't mess with us. We're going to do this story, one way or another. And we don't really need you. We're just being nice. We're giving you a chance to go up against somebody else and prove your cre-a-tiv-i-ty."

Yeah, right! Like I believed that crap!

– 3 –

I WENT HOME AND BEGAN reading Jane Austen. I knew it would take all weekend to finish her books. My cell phone kept ringing all through *Pride and Prejudice* but I ignored it. My stomach growled during *Sense and Sensibility*—I ignored that, too.

Before I began *Mansfield Park* I ran a lovely bath, threw in lavender bubble stuff, opened a bottle of Chardonnay (someone gave it to me last Christmas), poured a glass, and put it on a tray along with Brie cheese, crackers, and grapes.

I felt like a dusty scholar seeking clues from ancient scrolls. Yes, I was looking for universal knowledge.

Reading Jane Austen taught me to look for serious consequences from simple things. Everything that happens to a person is important.

Her books illustrate how everyday lives can be heroic, how

silly conversations and flirtations can lead to great insight . . . and how that insight can change lives.

I know some people think her books are silly because they focus on love and marriage.

I disagree.

Nothing is more important to Jane than love of family, of country, of a mate.

But Jane knows a few things . . .

Sometimes love hurts.

Other times it injures severely.

Most times, love is savage.

— 4 —

OKAY.

But how to apply Jane's standards in a world where celebrity and scandal dominate?

— 5 —

LET'S BE HONEST.

All my life I wanted to be in the film business, because that's what Dad did. And now before me was my innermost dream (competing with my fantasy of bedding down a certain Lad).

Even my career as a film critic had been plotted by me to open those Hollywood doors. Odd that they'd been opened, not by my professional efforts, but by a silly little film that my darling mom had gone basic for.

So, here was an opportunity to die for.

But the bottom line was that I couldn't cause my mother any pain. The right thing to do was to see my mom, talk over this situation with her, and then come to some conclusion.

But even as I decided to do the *right* thing, to behave as a proper Austen person, my heart kept beating to a more primal rhythm:

> *This is your chance . . .*
> *Take it, stupid!*
> *Don't be an asshole!*
> *Don't be a silly schoolgirl!*
> *Be a player!*
> *Be cool!*

Chapter Nineteen

❧

— 1 —

THREE DAYS LATER I EMERGED, steeped in the Austen sensibility, when men and women bowed to each other and proper English was used to communicate. And then they married.

I checked my messages. No English there.

Harry: "Hey, luv, give me a toot!"

Trumbull: "Chickie-baby, time is running out."

Sam Shapiro: "Need to talk to you, kid."

A couple of weirdos. "I'd like to. . . ."

Ugh.

Then, the telemarketing recordings offering free vacations, free life insurance, free Internet service.

I deleted all that.

Then Fancy, saying she was coming over with the NYPD if I didn't call her soon.

Tony, with an apology for coming on to me. Said he must've been mentally challenged that day.

Edgar, announcing the JANO meet tomorrow night.

Bitsy Zachary, thanking me for my wedding gift. "But Lizzie, it's quite vulgar."

(It was.)

But no message from Mom. That worried me.

I checked my e-mails. There, too, the usual spam nonsense. Did I want a BIGGER PENIS? Why was my mortgage rate so high? Did I need better skin products? Was my soul going to hell?
Ugh.
The life of a jane in Manhattan can be hell sometimes.

− 2 −

USUALLY, I DIDN'T OPEN e-mails with addresses unknown to me—in the event there was a virus. But then I saw one with the e-mail address—HARRY'S EX!
Oh-oh!
Here we go . . .
It began:

```
You poor darling,
     Join the adoring Harry exes gang. There
are many of us. We all thought we'd land
handsome Harry. But our residences ran
from one to six months.
     I lasted till one morning Harry said
he needed interiors. So we went shop-
ping. What I didn't know is that Harry
meant to change me, as well.
     The next time he drops you on that
great oak table in the solarium, I want
you to remember that I picked that out for
Harry. So when he bends you over the
```

```
expensive  oak  and  tells  you  he  loves
you . . .
    DO think of me.
    I want to warn you that it probably
means you're good to go.
Best wishes,
Stella—a Harry Ex-Girlfriend
```

I couldn't believe it. Just when I was trusting Harry, I learn that he has an entire group of former flames?

Of course I called him immediately.

"Darling . . ." his voice was sweet and low.

"Who's Stella?" I demanded.

"Stella who?"

"Don't be smart with me, Harry. Stella, the girlfriend who picked out the oak table in your solarium."

"Oh, *that* Stella. We dated for a while."

"I *know* that already. What else?"

I was trying to be as much like a Mother T as I could remember from Twinkie's description. What did she say? *Stomp his stuff and stay soo calm.* Good advice.

"Look, Lizzie. I wasn't born yesterday. Yes, I've had a few girlfriends before you."

"And Stella?"

"She was one of the weird ones. Can't let go. Still calls me in the middle of the night and wants to come over."

Smoke the man!

"She's never called when *I* was there."

"Lizzie, you haven't ever had a sleepover. You always jump up and run home for the eleven o'clock news." He paused. "Or so you say."

"Don't you believe me? You've slept at my place and know I MUST watch the eleven P.M. news. As a matter of fact, you've watched with me."

"Hey, what's wrong, sweetheart? I thought we were in a nice place at last."

A Mother T makes her man writhe with pain.

"Don't call me sweetheart. I'm *not* your sweetheart. I'll *never* be your sweetheart."

"Why are you acting like this? Are you on some kind of medication?"

She sticks her pins into him.

"I received a very upsetting e-mail from your Stella. She says that there's a gang of your exes out there just ready to pounce and save me from your clutches!!"

"Hell. I had to get a restraining order on Stella. She's bonkers!"

A Mother T is a real zinger, sweet and hard at the same time!

I pitched my voice low and sexy now. "Okay, Harry. I believe you."

His voice relaxed. "Well, that's better. Will I see you tonight?"

A Mother T gives him a foot right in the place he treasures the most—his big COCK!!!

"Sorry. I'm busy."

A pause. I heard him breathing hard.

"Is that any way to treat the guy who adores you?"

"Things are racing ahead—I have to think about all of this—and about your firing me—"

"I didn't fire you. Ron did."

"You could've saved my gig."

"I have other plans for you. I want to tell you about them, if we ever get together without histrionics."

Mother T knows how to smoke him bad.

"It was nice of you to keep my name out of the gossip columns," I said sweetly.

"I want to be with you, Lizzie. Are you listening to me?"

She's just testing him to see if he's a REAL man.

"Let's wait and see how it all shakes out. I need some private time—got things to deal with. Sorry, Harry. I'll call you."

"Damn bitch!" I heard him mutter as he slammed the phone in my ear.

— 3 —

I GUESS HE WAS MAD. Well, this girlfriend wasn't going to end up like the other exes in his collection. This girlfriend would play the wait-and-see game. Let's just compute what Harry will come up with next in his courtship.

I was confident. I'd just read six Jane Austen books and knew this was the way for a heroine to go.

Hadn't Fitzwilliam Darcy apologized after being arrogant and overbearing (though *veree* sexy) to Elizabeth for most of *Pride and Prejudice*?

Elizabeth simply stood by her principles until Darcy proposed.

An excellent strategy—and one I planned to follow.

IT WAS ABOUT TIME!

Too many men had mucked me over . . . now it was my turn.

Be strong, be swift, be lethal!

Yes, that was it. I had to incorporate a little *Mother T* into my *veree* civilized Jane personality.

I had to stop being a pushover for any man who looked like my Darling Lad and aim for the main man, who just happened to be appearing at the Metro Film Festival next week—which I'd been invited to attend.

But now that Ron had yanked my treasured press pass, would the invite be shredded?

Oh, hell.

— 4 —

MOM'S OFFICE LOOKED LIKE a tornado zone. Manuscripts and papers were tossed all over the floor. Books were haphazardly piled beside large, half-filled cartons. Plastic cups, spoons, knives, forks, pens, pencils, paper clips, were strewn about like confetti.

On the floor next to five pairs of New Balance shoes were the components of Mom's expensive computer, along with various connecting wires and boards.

Oddly, the photographs on the wall were still in place. They were old photos of an advertising campaign. The collection consisted of smokily glamorous black-and-white portraits of stars like Marlene and Sophia, dating from the Sixties.

The sight of those icons draped in animal pelts startled me. Why had Mom collected these advertisements? Maybe they put her in touch with her kooky childhood, when she'd come home from Catholic school to find Gran and her showbiz cronies having their martini lunches and exchanging naughty stories about their lives and loves whilst working in the Broadway theater.

Grandmother Alice had a good half-dozen fur coats in her closet. In fact, one of her favorite performance pieces was dancing nude with a sable wrapped round her body.

I planned, one day, to wear the very same thing during my first invitation to my Darling Lad's apartment.

Unfortunately, this was a silly fantasy. I was now *against* all fur coats because of my animal-rights convictions.

But those were not Mom's feelings, another area where we

were different. Mom wore fur whenever she possibly could. She said it made her feel loved.

I dunno. Women are such strange creatures. Unlike men, who need REAL sex, ladies get hot over a fur coat or, as is well known, Manolo Blahnik footwear.
Guess we learn how to substitute early.

$$- 5 -$$

MOM SAT WITH HER BACK to the door, looking out at the campus. She seemed slumped over in an odd position.
"What's up?" I tried to sound cheerful.
When she turned, Mom's eyes were shadowed, her lips were glossed. Her hair was untamed and worn slightly to one side. She looked so intense, I knew there was something dark going on.
Had the gossip gotten to her, I asked.
She sat up straight and threw back her hair. "It's payback time," she said angrily, hauling a pile of books from the desk and setting them by my feet. When I retrieved the teetering pile, I was startled to see they were her bestsellers.
"Mom?"
"Lizzie, be warned. When you're a woman who tells the truth, people think of you as a she-devil. I've always had to field character assassinations. I've gone to lunch at *Le Cirque* and women in silly hats have whispered about me. I've received crank letters about all sorts of sexual goings-on.
"And like women before me who speak out honestly, when attacked, I kept my mouth shut. But now I'm going to sue the

bastards. To hell with grace under pressure and all that gentle-men's agreement nonsense."

"You can't sue the media, Mom. Your nude spot is on film. You can't fight that."

"Not the media, the university." She took a deep breath. "They fired me. All my rebel pals backed the chairman of our department. They're really enjoying those pretty white houses in the Hamptons and couldn't afford to have a fuss."

"What about your contract?"

"They're buying me out. I'll be fine as far as money goes, but it's the principle of the thing."

I went round to her and put my arm about her bent shoulders. "Don't worry, Mom. You don't need the university."

"Oh, yes, I do. You don't know how the world works, do you, darling?"

"I . . .

"I haven't told you everything you need to know. I wanted you to tackle the world and tell them all to shove it."

"Mom, don't go on like this."

She waved me away. "I taught you about being smart and not taking shit from anyone. And about sex, and about using condoms. About being independent and making it on your own. But maybe I was wrong not to warn you—there's always the piper to pay."

She looked much too hurt, too despairing. "I wasn't always honest with you, darling. But I wanted you to be fearless."

I'd never known her to respond this way. On the day Mom told me that Dad was leaving, she just ploughed on with a rock-like determination and said that we'd have to move because we didn't have much money and didn't need all that space anyhow.

Even as I cried for my father, I thought my mother had remarkable courage.

My spirits fell as I watched her eyes grow misty. "You're so like your father. Nick is an incurable romantic. He loves film stars and films, just the way you do."

I choked up at her use of the present tense.

"The thing is, Lizzie—" She looked so incredibly frightened, I feared for her reason.

She rummaged through her shoulder bag and pulled out a crumpled letter. "I have something for you. It arrived this morning."

I took it from her. It was handwritten in a shaky scrawl. But all I saw was the return address.

```
Nick Blakely
100 Mission Street
San Francisco, CA
```

Chapter Twenty

— 1 —

"**I**'M NOT SURE YOU should read that," Mom said.

When I shook my head in disagreement, she added, "Okay, but don't say you weren't warned."

Her face wore an expression of guarded sympathy for me, but her eyes reflected too much hurt. As I folded the letter into my purse, she was ever watchful—as if the contents would suddenly explode.

"I'm sorry, Mom."

She offered no helping hand to me, as well as no redemption for my Dad. Instead, she masked her anguish, as usual, in high-toned comments.

"Why in heaven is Nick suddenly writing to you? What does he have to say? All these years, he's ignored you. Oh, my poor Lizzie, darling . . . I don't want you to be hurt again."

"Mom, I'd rather read this when I'm alone. Do you mind?"

I could see it in her eyes that she did, but she said, "Of course not. I understand."

So I went home.

— 2 —

I SNUGGLED INTO THE WINDOW SEAT which gave me a private, though minuscule, glimpse of the Hudson River. Just then, an elegant cruise ship sailed by.

From my narrow vantage point, I watched it pass bit by bit, not able to see its entirety.

I realized that was how my life was revealed to me, in tiny bits.

With trembling hands, I opened the envelope. The stationery was cheap, almost tissue thin. It was the type that was sold to imitate the good stuff, but instead sent a message of the sender's shame.

Inside, on lined pad paper, my father's message was written in red ink which often smudged. There were small red blots and large ones. Some looked like broken hearts.

`My darling Princess,`

That's what Dad always called me. I looked out the window, parted the soft white curtain that had loosened from its ties, and closed my eyes.

The smell of jam, peanut butter, and toasted coarse whole wheat bread enveloped me. I would watch Dad butter the toast and giggle when he pretended that he would hog it for his own. Our breakfast ritual—another thing I'd forgotten.

— 3 —

My darling Princess,

   I'm terribly sorry that I haven't
been part of your life. But I've thought
of you every day and every moment. Your
sweet face is always before me. On my
desk I have a lovely photo of you.

Until recently, I'd had Dad's photo at my bedside. Where
was it now? I looked around the room, expecting it to pop out
of its hiding place. It didn't.

— 4 —

THE ROOM WAS FILLED with a strange silence and as I read
on, my father's voice seemed to narrate the written words.

   When I left New York, I was very ill.
I drank my way across the country and
landed in San Francisco an alcoholic.
Now I've recovered.
   I just learned about your mother's
difficulties and feel responsible.
   What can I do to help?

My heart beat so wildly I had to put the letter down. I

jumped up and swiftly walked to my door, grabbed my purse, and exited.

On the other side of the door, my name was engraved on a brass plate: Elizabeth Parsons.

But it should read Elizabeth Blakely.

So I went back inside.

— 5 —

```
     Lizzie, I know you can never forgive
me for leaving you and your Mom. It must
have been terrible for you. But I'm ask-
ing you to regard that as the act of a
very sick man.
     I also know I hurt you, and you've
probably paid the price.
     Can you forgive me for not being
there for you?
     Will you let me make amends?

                                     Dad
```

Under a few red blots, he'd scrawled,

```
I love you.
```

At first I wept a storm of hard tears.

I felt I was entering a familiar dream, walking in a garden with rose bushes. Feverishly I grasped the blossoms, only to be pricked by the thorns.

Watch out for thorns, I warned my heart.

Now, while reading my father's words, old wounds reopened.

When I recalled my mother's anguish . . .

When I remembered our phone-call ritual . . .

And I realized that during the dangerous summer he left us, I'd lost my bearings as well as my heart.

So I tore up the letter into tiny little pieces and stomped on them.

Chapter Twenty-one

— 1 —

I WOKE UP ANGRY, tossed on sweat pants, a T-shirt, donned track shoes, and left home in a hurry. I went to the waterfront and ran two miles north, than back again. Sweaty, I stopped at the Caffé Rosetta for breakfast, where I ordered all the wrong things. Cappuccino topped with whipped cream. French toast steeped in Vermont syrup. Afterwards, a slice of mocha cake.

Back home, I felt like upchucking. Instead, I took two Tums, showered, and spent the entire day working on my screenplay. But my temper was out of control, and I couldn't focus. So I poured a double Scotch, slugged it down, and took a nap.

When I awoke, it was teatime, only I didn't feel much like tea. It was also time for the JANO meeting. I ran a bath, filled the tub with sea salts left over from my courtesan lesson, and soaked for a half-hour before I felt like myself again, whoever that was.

I knew what I had to do.

Oh, Gawd!

– 2 –

"THIS IS THE HARDEST THING I've ever done. I'm quitting JANO," I abruptly announced to my fellow JANO-ites and then burst into a storm of tears.

The other members looked disturbed by my unusual behavior. I was usually the smart girl, the one with all the answers and all the quips. And now I was acting like any ol' soap heroine, crying into my coffee, so to speak.

My Jane Austen marathon had a side effect. It brought forth a memory I wanted to suppress. And, in my current hysteria, if I began sharing with my fellow JANO-ites, I knew I'd blurt it out.
They couldn't help me. Nobody could.
Because I had a secret—something I was hiding.

Gabe's hotel room was generally noisy, but now it was hushed. Our host sat forward on an exercise bicycle built for two, his mouth opened in a wide O. Dear Edgar folded his slim, well-manicured hands into a prayer mode. Bonnie Bolton's eyes were filled with tears. (She was a former JANO-ite who'd recently rejoined the club.) Her daughter, Pauline Dorsey, wore wispy French bangs, frizzled now from the sweat on her brow.

And Fancy's pal, Dottie Sutton Matrix, sat with her legs crossed in a *veree* erotic pose, which she said was the most relaxing position she'd discovered in her many years as a dancer.

"But, Lizzie . . ." she protested.

I cut her off. "Jane simply isn't helping me. My life is shit. I have no gig. Mom is going to court, which will mean more naked pictures of her all over TV." My throat constricted, so I had to force out my words. "And my new squeeze, Harry, is a misogynist. There's actually a club of exes for the man. And most of all—most of all—" my voice started shaking, "my missing Dad is back."

"Your dad?" Bonnie Bolton said. "I know I've missed a lot of meetings, but have you mentioned him before?"

I felt my cheeks flush. "Never had to. He's not part of my life. But he wants to be in it now. He sent me a note with lots of sincerity in it." I scowled. "He probably needs cash or a bank loan, but he damn well is not going to get it from me!"

I picked up my empty coffee mug and threw it across the room. It shattered under the minuscule altar Gabe had concocted since he began studying the Kabbala and reflecting on God.

"Hey, stop acting like a brat!" he said, climbing down from his bicycle to pick up the pieces.

"I *am* a brat. I will *always* be a brat. I *intend* to be a brat for the rest of my whole fucking life!" I yelled.

"Hardly the response of an Austen Girl," Edgar said sardonically as he unfolded his hands and quietly reached for the vodka.

"Don't do that, Edgar," I cried.

But he poured one, then another. All of us knew that for Edgar Meredith this meant it was crisis time.

— 3 —

THROUGH MY TEARS, I saw that the attendees at JANO looked astounded, but it was Bonnie who delicately tried to probe my distress. "Tell us about your dad."

Instantly, I babbled. "I never told you this, but I really missed my dad all these years, and I blamed Mom for his absence. Now I definitely know she was crazy."

"We were all crazy back then. It was normal," BB said.

"I used to think so. But that was before I knew about Mom's nude film. Probably some amateur filmmaker talked her into it. And Mom's wide-eyed naivete didn't help."

"Look, we weren't as smart as you New Girls in those days," BB said.

"Okay. But where was Dad in all this? Was he on the sidelines egging her on? That's what Mom hinted. So what kind of man does that? Only a hustler, right?"

Edgar laughed. "This is news? Your dad worked for Sam Shapiro, the Great Hustler Mentor of the Seventies. If Nick lasted more than a day with Sam, he must have been pretty sharp."

"So he was good at his job," I conceded. "But he wasn't good as a dad."

"That's probably why he ended up a drunk. But it seems he's changed. That's why you must show your dad some compassion," Edgar said adamantly.

I shook my head stubbornly, so he raised his glass to continue drinking. His lips twisted as he said, "I'm an alcoholic. Those of us who get sober go through the Twelve-Step Program. Among them is a step about making amends. Your dad is probably up to that one."

"Yeah," said Gabe while the group nodded in unison.

"What do you know about this?" I asked.

Gabe's head bent and he looked ashamed. "We have the same step program at SAC."

"SAC?" BB asked.

"Sexual Addiction Counseling."

$$- 4 -$$

GABE EXPLAINED, "I HAVEN'T been truthful with all of you." He blushed oddly as he continued. "I'm a sex addict."

"Huh?"

I was vetting my memory for a hint of Gabe's problem. All the while I dated him, I thought he was simply a player, a typical cocksman in the New York scene. But now he was confessing to a serious obsession.

"It happens to me all the time. Last week, I was sitting on a bench in Central Park when a woman sat down next to me and put her hand on my thigh. She was older, a woman of a certain age. She wore golden earrings, and her fingers were heavily jeweled. When we walked down the path I saw that other men were admiring her dark brown eyes and big, soft lips. So we came here . . ."

Gabe gestured to the bedroom. "And we stayed in bed for a week. We ate take-out, watched TV and DVDs, and we fucked and fucked. By the end of the week she wanted to meet my friends, and I don't know what to do about it. Because all I want is sex from her . . . from all of them. I don't want anything else!"

"Oh, shove that," Rick said. "Just grow up and be a man."

"And what is a man?" Dottie chipped in.

"He's someone who doesn't cry in public," Edgar repeated his mantra between sips of vodka.

"Nor does he masturbate there," Dottie quipped.

— 5 —

I FOUND ALL OF THIS *veree* disturbing.

My fragile poise crashed, and a new storm of tears flooded my face. I was making a goddamn fool of myself.

"I'm going home." I made a beeline for the door, but Gabe blocked my way.

"No. Sit down, we're going to help you through this."

I looked at him. "No, thanks!"

"Come back," Edgar called softly. "We love you, Lizzie. We're your pals."

I returned to the group, but I was not comfortable, so I joked. "I am acting a bit like Bridget Jones, aren't I?"

Everyone laughed, and I felt better. Damn. I didn't mind hearing their problems. But mine, oh hell!

Dottie laughed. "Oh, my! What would dear Jane think of us?"

"Her people were into money and class," Pauline commented.

"We're still into that," Edgar said. "And then there's all the other silly stuff about LOVE."

– 6 –

EDGAR'S REMARK MADE ME REALIZE that for a man (even a Jane Austen man), love was difficult. And if men were stoic about love, how the hell could we ladies know how they really felt?

Yet I suspected that underneath all this rah-rah stuff, Edgar, Tony, and probably Harry were totally threatened by their feelings. With the male edict of never letting tears show, it's no wonder they played the love game so unfairly.

So I said, "But if men won't weep, and women do nothing but weep, we can never get together."

"Maybe we aren't meant to stay together," BB said. "I've been divorced five times, and I've never been happier than now, living alone."

"But OUR JANE venerated the idea of the family. She wouldn't approve of divorce," I insisted.

"When did your parents go through theirs?" Edgar suddenly asked me.

I felt my heart beat faster as I planned to lie. But it didn't work. "They were never divorced," I whispered.

Oh, no. My secret was slipping out.

"They're still married?" Gabe said eagerly.

"No. They were *never* married." I could feel the shame burning across my face. "In Jane's world I'd be called a bastard."

There was a strained silence.

"But not in our world," Edgar said softly. "Lizzie, I've known you for quite some time, and you've never mentioned this. Are you ashamed of it?"

My lips quivered. "I guess . . ."

Gabe spoke quickly. "Hey, nobody's parents are great. My mother was a shoplifter, even though she had every major credit card in her purse. Do you know how many times I had to rescue her from the Fifth Avenue stores? She'd spend hours dressing up in Dior for her courtroom appearances. Loved the attention."

BB asked Gabe, "Did she go to jail?"

"No. My father jumped in to bail her out. He opened up store charge accounts and put money in them so everything she stole was paid for."

"My dad had three mistresses," Pauline said, while BB frowned.

"My father liked to hunt," Rick said. "That's why I became a priest."

"Everyone's parents suck," Edgar said benevolently. "Except the exceptionally lucky children who appeared in Hollywood films during the Fifties."

I laughed. "Thanks for making me feel better about it."

Rick, the ex-priest, sermonized. "Lizzie, remember that

Jane Austen wants us to rise above difficulty and take life's negativity in our stride."

Edgar added, "Elizabeth Bennet said, 'I'm a gentleman's daughter.' You must remember you're a rebel's daughter. Maggie is quite a courageous woman."

"Oh, shit! Stop wallowing in self-pity, Lizzie! Step out and do the dance!" Dottie said impatiently. "That's what Jane Austen really wants us to do!"

"Hear, hear!" from the JANO chorus.

"You're not going to quit us, are you?" Gabe said sweetly.

I looked at their hopeful faces and was touched.

"Guess not," I said.

The funny thing is that I always treated our Jane Austen club with irony, just as Jane had treated her society.

But I had to remember that under all that humor, Jane always cared deeply for people.

And I guess I do, too.

It was nice to see they sort of cared about me, as well.

Chapter Twenty-two

— 1 —

WHEN I LEFT THE MEETING, I felt relieved. My secret was out, and instead of experiencing shame, I was feeling quite on top of things. But there was more to be done. The JANO meeting had convinced me that Dad was seeking forgiveness from Mom and me.

I had to plead his case. Here was a chance to heal the past.

Still, the fact that Dad hadn't married Mom—or vice versa—gnawed at my heart.

— 2 —

I LEARNED I WAS A BASTARD when Mitzi Simmons, whose mother was the neighborhood gossip, shouted the word at me after I'd gotten the lead in our school play, *The Princess.*

I was so excited. When Mrs. Stapleton told me I was to be the princess, I burst into happy tears. On my way home, I dreamt about the pretty dress I'd wear, wondered if Gran would lend me a piece of her incredible sparkling jewelry, and hoped Mom would let me wear satin shoes.

That's when Mitzi and her crew pounced on me. From the ground, I looked up at the face of female jealousy, something I now know how to identify.

"You don't deserve to be the princess. You're a sinner."

This from a daughter of a Greenwich Village hipster?

"We're Catholic, we're allowed to sin." I spat out the words with pride.

(Mom had explained that Catholics were allowed to sin and ask for forgiveness.)

"My mom says you're a bastard. Your parents aren't married." Mitzi mocked me.

I went home sobbing when I should've been happy. The moment I saw my mother, I blurted out what happened and asked if it was true.

Mom took me aside and said that she and Dad were very much in love and hadn't gotten married because they wanted to make a political statement. She said that when two people were so passionate, their love should be free of restrictions.

Mom said that love was a political act.

When Dad came home and saw my distress, he warmed up my favorite chocolate drink and told me to get ready for bed. When he joined me, he said, "Lizzie, if you're upset about Mom and I not marrying . . . suppose we do?"

I sipped the hot drink slowly. "Mom said it was important for you *not* to be married."

"Princess . . ." he kissed my forehead . . . "the most important thing is for you to be happy. Tell you what—I'll take Mom out to dinner, bring her flowers, get down on my knees, and ask her properly. Would you like that?"

I giggled. "And will she wear a white dress?"

He smiled. "The dress isn't important, Lizzie. What's important is that we all love each other."

That night I had happy dreams.

I don't know what happened because no one spoke about it, but I assumed Mom refused Dad's proposal. That's when our life began falling apart. Dad arrived later and later each night, only to be confronted by Mom's accusations.

Then he left.

And I always wondered whether it was my fault.

— 3 —

WHEN SHE CAME TO THE DOOR, Mom had a plastic mask over her face and wore a tight rubber corset which she claimed could reduce five percent of one's body fat. The aroma of Italian sauce wafted from the kitchen. I checked it out and saw a large tray of meatballs engulfed in the stuff.

That's when I knew Mom was in trouble. Vanity and cuisine were Mom's two main therapies.

"Is this a good time?" I asked, noting piles of legal papers on the table, probably the university court case.

"Darling," she said, "have a *polpetto.*"

"Are we going to be Italian today?"

"They're fun people, and we need some fun—don't we, darling?"

But she didn't look as if she were having much fun. So I asked, "Mom, are you upset because Dad wrote me?"

The clear plastic covering Mom's face couldn't hide her tears. "Yes," she said. "I'm afraid I'll lose you. You always adored Nick."

"Dad just wants to help."

"I don't *need* his help. I'll *never* need his help."

"Mom, couldn't you just be a *little* friendly?"

"Haven't I taught you anything, Lizzie?" she cried. "Never trust anyone who betrays you!"

"But Dad's an alcoholic. He's doing The Twelve-Step Program and wants to make amends. We can't condemn him for that, can we?"

She sat down, folded her arms, and eyed me warily.

I tried to be gentle. "I know Dad was unfaithful to you. And I know he left us. But he was sick. Can't we give him some slack?"

"Hey, that sounds really wonderful—like a self-help-how-to-forgive book. But that isn't how life is."

"And how is life?" I prodded.

"Life is about how fragile I felt all the while I was carrying you, and Gran paid all the bills. And after Gran died, how we went through the money she left us. Life is about how Nick wanted to work in the damn film business, and how I had to work as a waitress and then come home and take care of you. Life is about how working for Sam destroyed your father's principles until he became the kind of man I hate."

"So you tormented him until he left?"

"I don't know what I did, Lizzie. It's all a bad dream, and I don't want that dream back. That's why I can't talk to Nick. Can you understand that?"

When I didn't respond, an odd expression came over her face. "I've been very selfish, Lizzie. The best a mother can do is give it all she's got and hope that her kids turn out okay." Then she tossed her head and wrinkled her brow. "I know you miss Nick, but he's been away a long time. He's not the father you knew."

I blurted, "But I want to know who he is."

She looked puzzled. "Why now?"

I wasn't sure. But I knew I didn't want to live in Mom's angry world. That world was in the past. I wanted to be in love with Harry and make it work.

She must have read my mind. "Something's happened. You're in love, is that it?" She brightened. "Who is it, Lizzie? Tell me about him."

I realized that Adrienne had been true to her word. She hadn't told Mom about my seduction plan for Harry.

Good girl!

"There is someone, Mom. But the whole thing is up and down, around . . . and then some."

"That's how relationships are, Lizzie."

"I guess . . ."

She grasped my hand. "Look, don't worry about me. I'll be fine. You go ahead and do whatever you need to do." She blew me a kiss. "Just remember, I'm on your side, and I'll root for you."

"Really?"

"Yes, really."

Then she bit her lip and looked pensive—the way she did when she gave advice.

"Who is this guy? Does he look like your Brit?"

Oh-oh!

Here it comes.

"Yes, he does."

"Then he does have a chance with my Lizzie, doesn't he?"

"Maybe . . . but my Darling Lad is so gorgeous, so smart, so sexy."

"On film, he is. But you've never met him in the flesh. If he's that important to you, you really have to discover the man behind the roles, don't you?"

Oh, Gawd.
She'll never stop!

Chapter Twenty-three

❦

— 1 —

"**W**HERE THE HELL you been, girlfriend?" Fancy's outburst cut across the din at the Sugar Shop, where gossip was constant and like an opera, had its highs and lows.

The place resembled a fashion show. Tall, skinny waitresses walked about in sarong skirts and bare midriffs, dazzling customers whilst carrying egg-and-bacon sandwiches to the tables. Each one of them looked like the classic Greek and Roman statues of Venus.

"They should've called this the Venus Shop," I quipped. "All these girlfriends are gorgeous."

"Yup. But we can compete."

"Can we?"

"You sure can. I've never seen you looking so gor-ge-ous."

Actually I was—though I was paying for it. My gray snakeskin pants were much too tight, and though they accomplished their goal—my derriere was bound up tightly and terribly visual—the hip-hugging waistband dug deeply into my flesh. I tried not to mind, knowing I wore black lace undies in case partial nudity became my costume.

For a top, I wore a grey silk tee with ten tiny pearl buttons down the front. The first one was undone, and the next one would reveal the swell of my breasts. I'd shot my wallet on a trip to the Ritz Salon for a remarkable coif. As a result, my dark hair swirled about in ways that were astonishing— a little like Farrah Fawcett in the original *Charlie's Angels*.

"I've rarely seen you look so smashing," Fancy repeated. "Does this have something to do with the fact that a certain Brit is going to appear at the Metro Festival?" She giggled.

But I had a problem about the festival. "Were you able to get it?" I asked.

"Ron won't budge. I told him, I said, 'You can't expect our girlfriend, the great film critic, to go to this event like a civilian. It's not proper. It's *not done*.' But Ron said that you broke all rules of friendship and colleague decorum, so he will not give you your press pass back."

"Ever?"

"Never. But you can use mine."

"Thanks, but the regular press isn't allowed anymore. Only film critics are invited. Besides, Ron would freak out."

"Okay. I have another idea."

"And that is?"

"When are you going to get another gig?"

Guiltily, I bent my head. "I know. I know. I haven't been too smart about that. I'll start making calls tomorrow."

"Do it, girl. Don't take this lying down. Ron has been badmouthing you all over the place."

"Hell!"

"Don't worry. You have your fans." She paused, then added, "Besides, I have another idea that will solve our current problem."

"What's that?"

"Raoul Ryder's film is the first film being screened. Raoul is a former flame, so I called him this morning and begged him, simply begged him, to let you into his screening. He finally said he'd put your name on the list."

"Thanks. But that won't get me into tonight's gala."

"Girlfriend! It'll get you inside the festival. The rest will be up to your beauty and smarts."

Then she kissed me on both cheeks

– 2 –

THE METRO FESTIVAL IS New York City's answer to the fact that Los Angeles steals much of its former thunder. The powers that be are really angry because so many awards shows are now on the Coast.

Because influential film people live here, an impressive group of producers and performers insisted that Manhattan *must* reclaim its rightful place as the Center of the Arts.

In the past, remarkable writers and actors had worked in live television, then went out to Hollywood to become multimillionaires and renowned producers.

Everybody in the media knew that the Metro Festival wouldn't put a dent in international events like the Cannes Film Festival. But many thought since the strong American indie market, so important these days in movieland, was rooted in the East Coast, it should be publicized here.

Of course, major studios had bought up most of the indies, so one could hardly tell what was really an independent film and what wasn't.

But Raoul Ryder's *Chaos* had been made on a shoestring budget, so it obviously was. At various world festivals, it had already won the Director's Award, which meant that Raoul was coming into the Metro with his ego sky-high.

It was a well-publicized event. Many stars were billed to attend, among them My Darling Lad, who was in New York to publicize his latest film.

When I walked into the Wellsman Auditorium, where *Chaos* was being screened, I stood in the longish line headed by a pert girl checking names on a sheet.

I was fidgeting badly when Sam Shapiro walked by and spotted me. "Why are you on line, Lizzie?"

"Lost my press pass."

"What?" he asked, his voice a bit too loud.

"Lost my press pass," I repeated quietly.

"Come along with us. Justin," he waved to one of his entourage. "Take care of this."

I said, "Can't do that, Sam."

"You're being weird."

"I'm looking for a new gig. I can't join your party, because I'll have to review your future films."

"Don't be silly. I wiped your ass when you were a baby."

"That may be so." Then I blurted, "I heard from Dad."

His eyes shot open. "Nick! Where the hell is he? That guy is one of the best producers who ever worked for me."

"San Francisco."

"Is he a monk, or a hipster, or a twelve-stepper?"

He'd covered all the bases. "The last."

"If he's sober and wants a job, tell Nick to come back to Sam's family." Then he kissed me on the cheek. "Sure you don't want to join us?"

He knew I did and continued tempting me. "If you give up this critic gig, you can read scripts for me. Or write some. Wouldn't you like that? Huh?" He put his finger under my chin and tickled me the way he had when I was a little girl.

I really did want that. He was talking about one of my fantasies.

On a more urgent level, Sam would probably sit in the VIP section with its plush sofas. Nice. And there would be champagne, and chopped egg and cucumber sandwiches (Sam was a big Anglophile), and people would be fussing over him.

That's because Sam Shapiro had the ability to surround himself with talented colleagues who fueled his ambition and entrepreneurship. One of his producers was a former high school pal. The head of the publicity department was married to one of his daughters. The art director was someone he'd met at NYU back when he studied film.

Sam liked the idea of an extended family always somewhere nearby, working, talking, joking, fighting. The Shapiro Film Family was important to Sam, and he hated it when he lost a member, like my dad, Nick Blakely.

And now Sam wanted me in his family, as well.

But it simply wouldn't do. I was a film critic, damn it, not a hanger-on.

And though *The Village Record* had begun as a community-oriented paper concentrating on local politics and the arts, it had grown in stature—spiffy enough to recruit people like Harry, who'd worked on several major newspapers.

Admittedly, I was at the bottom of the food chain as a free-lancer, but management provided me with a press pass and printed my reviews faithfully. I'd thought the next step was to be put on staff. Instead I found myself fired.

Though the field was crowded with wannabes, I had forged a reputation. As soon as I get my act together, I'm sure I could snag another gig.

That's what I told myself as I waited in line, feeling morally smug.

— 3 —

I WASN'T FEELING TOO SMUG when I finally reached the tiny tot at the head of the line. "Elizabeth Parsons," I said.

She didn't look up in acknowledgment, busily scanning her list. At the bottom, someone had scrawled in my name.

"Enjoy the film." Still not looking, the girl handed me a program.

When I walked in, the place was almost filled. I spotted several prominent film people sitting with Sam's group. I took a seat in the rear and searched the audience for my Darling Lad. No luck. He was scheduled to be at the festival, but I wasn't privy as to where and when.

Chaos was one of the most talked-about films of a very mediocre season. This year, The Cannes Festival had not been too exciting, the judges calling most of the entries a hodgepodge of difficult, puzzling, boring, self-gratifying, and terrible films.

In this venue, *Chaos* had won several awards, so that now Raoul Ryder would instantly leap from an independent filmmaker, living on the Lower East Side and working tables at a local restaurant, to someone who could probably get a job at a university, receive invites to all private parties in this closed circle, and wangle appointments with studios to talk about projects.

The buzz in the audience was shrill. Several academic types were seated next to me. "The payoff from DVD sales for this year's action-adventure blockbusters is enormous," a guy in a wilted suit said. "And what about the teen comedies? They're over the top. I think the studios are using their DVD sales figures to discredit serious films."

His companion, wearing something that looked like a Day-Glo caftan, agreed. "If a film flops in the theaters due to bad reviews, there used to be nothing the studios could do. But now they're buying lamebrain caper movies, just because the DVD will sell."

"The last time we had good mainstream cinema was the Seventies. That's when you had the Coppola, the Scorsese, the Altman films with their offbeat, even shocking approaches," another academic in shorts and sandals added.

Was this news?

I'd been writing about the problem for the last two years. Where were those gorgeous films where an encounter could change a life and haunt a woman or a man forever? Where were the intimate films where relationships could be explored?

When Dad was working for Sam, the Europeans were doing this style of film, and the American studios, noting their profits, had plunged in.

But now it was all changed.

– 4 –

I COULDN'T LISTEN ANYMORE, so I put my hands over my ears. Fortunately the lights dimmed, and the projector began.

A half-hour into the film, I wanted to leave. Ryder had filmed a graphic anal sex scene that was unbearably humiliating for the female lead. (The rumor was that they were sleeping together, so it may even have been real.)

I'm happy to say that this New York media audience agreed with my assessment.

"This is shit!" someone in the first row yelled. Additional loud and angry shouts followed. Raoul Ryder, seated in a little alcove off to the side, stood up and gave the audience the finger.

Not smart.

The film continued as his protagonist had sex with a French housekeeper who worked for him, then his daughter's best friend, and. . . .

I'd had it.

– 5 –

FROM THE LOBBY, I SPOTTED several limousines at curbside. "Who's here?" I asked the super-handsome guy in an usher's uniform. He had that blond, cropped-hair look that usually distinguished people in the beauty business— probably an actor or model.

This cutie looked at me with disdain. "I can't really discuss it."

"I'm in the business," I stammered.

"Do you have press credentials?" he asked with a smirk.

"Not with me."

He glanced at me without mercy, his eyes going right through me

"The exit is there to the left," he said.

How the hell could he miss that I was someone important? For this dire emergency, I'd studied outfits worn by Julia. Didn't he recognize the look of a Media Goddess?

I'd even painted my nails a strange silver tone and worn high-heeled Roman sandals. I could try out for any diva role in this outfit—and probably get it!

Outside, I found a wall of bodies in every direction. Another gorgeous usher motioned for me to join the onlookers pressed behind loops of velvet rope dividing them from the auditorium entrance.

That's when I realized some held all-too-familiar Darling Lad posters.

Oh God!

It's HIM!

The ushers concentrated on pushing the crowd back and keeping the ropes solidly in place. I noticed two burly bodyguards near one of the entrances. They looked restless, so I knew their charge would be appearing imminently.

Okay.

I decided on bold movement, pushing past a large man holding a poster. He was a gentleman and moved away, but the fullback-sized woman with him swung her purse to smack me right on the noggin. I did a tango sidestep—Gabriel had taught me every possible tango maneuver during our affair. So she missed me. But she caught one of the burly bodyguards smack in the caboose.

The big man made a grab for the Fraulein (yes, she looked like a Nazi fullback), but she was too fast for him and disappeared into the sea of adoring fans.

Then the crowd let out a yell.

And there he was!

My heart did a flip-flop. My Darling Lad was wearing that naughty smile. Sweat rolled down my face. I was crazy. Around me, other fans looked equally nuts, all addicts who needed their fix—just as I did.

— 6 —

HE WALKED IN OUR DIRECTION and all around me, fans reached out to touch him. He smiled at them and politely greeted them, signing some autographs as he headed for the limo.

In front of me, two cuties were shoving their skimpily-clad bosoms at him, screaming his name.

Boldly, I did the same. One pearl button, then a second, and my lace bra was in view.

"Hi?" I called into the din as he passed quite near. (I felt like a hooker calling to a john.)

It worked. His darling blue eyes fluttered down to look at my assets. I waited with bated breath as he bent to whisper something, hopefully naughty.

But an awful blonde press person shoved me aside, saying, "We'd better move. We're falling behind schedule."

So he tore his eyes from me and was led away from the crowd's adoring bedlam.

As the crowd thinned, I watched the limo drive away. My heart felt broken. For my Darling Lad had looked at me as if I were just another ordinary, cute fan.

But I wasn't.

I was an intelligent, hard-working film critic who admired him professionally. And I vowed to continue.

That's when I knew that whatever I had to do to get my job back, I would do it.

I must do it.

Chapter Twenty-four

— 1 —

FILLED WITH MY NEW SENSE of purpose, I headed home. I must call Harry. Didn't he claim he had plans for me? Perhaps it was a new gig.

But I vowed to be utterly impersonal. The fact that Harry and I had ever shagged must have *no* place in this communication.

I had a cup of tea and dialed his office. "Harry's working at home today," Sally, the receptionist, said.

"Is he taking calls?" I went overboard here, wanting to make sure that she—and everyone she'd blab to—would understand this was a professional call.

"Yes, he is. Do you have his number?"

"Thank you, yes."

I certainly did have Harry's number—or, rather, numbers. I had one for his cell phone, though he turned that off when working. Then there was the number for his home phone— and for the private line in his bedroom. Knowing Harry liked to work in bed, I dialed the latter.

"Who is it?"

A female voice.

Damn Harry!

I slammed the phone down hard.

− 2 −

MY CHOICE WAS MORE TEA or Scotch. I went with the second option, even though booze made me sick. It was only three P.M. on a day when I'd first encountered my Darling Lad, and I was falling apart.

The reason was simple. I cared MUCH TOO MUCH!

I envied those movie stars who wore Jimmy Choos and became Buddhists—poster girls for remaining silent. These enigmatic mummies wore micro-mini skirts, went to fashionable Hamptons parties, and knew absolutely everything while maintaining a meditational hush before various Eastern icons.

In contrast, we *Sex and the City* girls got into difficulties.

As soon as we opened our mouths, we were in T-R-O-U-B-L-E!!!

Everything was evidence in the courtroom of male ego.

THE MALE DATING RULES:

1. A man needs his privacy
2. Don't ask a man questions
3. A man is always busy next weekend
4. Please leave this man alone!

− 3 −

THE PROBLEM IS THAT Gotham girls are passionate. Our friendships have a live-or-die element to them—and love affairs are even more intense.

This is how it goes. While I experience a spiritual and sensuous emotion when Harry tears off my bikini panties and bra, Harry only feels *enjoyment.*

After sex, most men join the Daniel Cleaver Club.

DANIEL CLEAVER CLUB RULES:

1. Avoid being intimate
2. As soon as possible, get back to the football game
3. No sleep-overs—plead an emergency at work
4. Be charming the next morning on the phone
5. Discuss potential date for HOT SEX
6. In emergencies—send flowers

BRIDGET JONES WAS CORRECT!!
Remember how awful she felt when discovering Daniel with that bronze American bitch!!
Well, after three drinks I was all set to storm the HARRY ARCHER bedroom.
Then I looked over at my bookshelves, at my JANE AUSTEN collection.
No. Aggressive behavior wasn't for me.
I was an Austen Girl, goddamn it!
And Austen Girls are ladies!
This meant I must dream up a Machiavellian scheme to punish Harry for being with another.
And that was about as far as I got before I fell asleep.

— 4 —

I WOKE UP WITH A FOUL taste in my mouth. No wonder I

didn't like whiskey—whiskey didn't like me. I managed to get to the fridge and drained the orange juice container dry.

I felt shitty. Stay away from booze, I chided myself. Remember Dad's illness.

I went back to the study, rummaged behind the encyclopedias, and found his photo. There he was . . . that handsome face, those lovely green eyes.

I picked up the phone and punched up San Francisco information. In a few seconds, I had his number.

Should I?

Or shouldn't I?

I decided I should.

"Hi, Dad," my voice sounded hesitant, almost timid.

"Princess, is it you?"

I told him everything. About Harry and my Darling Lad. About how I'd lost my gig and didn't seem to be doing anything to get another. And about Sam Shapiro's message for him.

"It's my fault," he said. "A girl needs a dad to spoil her. And I haven't done much of that, have I?"

"I . . ."

"It's okay. You can't say anything I haven't said to myself or at AA. Let me try to help."

He paused, then said, "You're hard on yourself. And you're awfully hard on your Harry. This guy cares for you. Give him a chance to explain."

"But what about this obsession I have with that bloody Brit?" I protested. "Isn't that sick?"

"Does Harry mind?"

"No, he laughs about it."

"So fly with it. That's what fantasies are for. I still have a crush on Audrey Hepburn."

"Did Mom mind?"

"She didn't mind about Audrey. But don't be like your mom and me . . . don't let love scare you. I did, and I paid for it dearly. Now I'm trying to get my life back together."

That's when he told me to get a gig. "Just call every media outlet."

"Okay," I agreed.

Then he asked me if I'd visit him.

I said maybe.

He said he loved me very much.

I said I'd definitely try.

"Good girl. So call Harry. Go for it!"

− 5 −

I DIDN'T HAVE TO, because Harry called me.

"Lizzie, why did you hang up when you called?"

Oh-oh. He had Caller ID!

Harry explained, "That was my housekeeper who answered."

Was this a Daniel Cleaver lie?

"I'm sorry, Harry. I thought . . ."

"I know what you thought. Look, I never know what you're up to, do I?"

Before I could answer, he continued. "Unless we have a commitment, it would be none of my business. Right?"

Good God! He was much more than a Daniel Cleaver genius. Harry was being positively Machiavellian.

But my father's advice warred with my suspicions.

Give the guy a break!

He could be telling the truth!

"I miss you, Harry," I said sweetly.

He sighed. "Lizzie, would you like to go to the Metro Festival Gala tonight?"

"You mean . . . ?"

"That's right," he laughed. "Your Lad will be there. I'll pick you up at eight. Okay?"

Totally okay!

But . . .

What on earth will I wear?

Chapter Twenty-five

— 1 —

THE REAL WORLD KEPT INTRUDING on my fantasy life.Could I strike up a tentative friendship with my Lad based on one introduction from tonight's gala? If I was lucky enough to be introduced to him, I wanted this British darling to remember me.

So how could I transform myself from an attractive New York media person to a FABULOUS *Sex and the City* minx?

This would take hard work. I examined the contents of my closet as if I were planning a prison break. It would be easy for me to do a downtown thing—remember my costume for Harry?

Still, the Lad might like a more elegant muse. Perhaps another version of downtown sexy? BLACK with sequined dominatrix touches?

How about uptown sexy? Beige shaded satin shirts and tweedy slit skirts and flats? Or is that too much like what the Brit girls wear—and thus, no mystery?

Society girl sexy? That involved Manolos and Gucci, which I couldn't afford.

Maybe television anchor sexy? Half-buttoned tailored shirt, buff suit, nice coif . . . or is that too boring?

Rock & roll sexy? Tight jeans with slashes, low-cut leather bodice, messy hair. A GOOD possibility.

OR . . . Jane Austen sexy? A clinging silk dress, matching spikes (not Manolos, I fear), tortoiseshell glasses, floppy hat. Nice choice.

I wanted to be terribly attractive, yet unusual, odd and perhaps a trifle forbidding. I could speak to my Darling Lad intellectually about films, hinting a sexuality that was about to break loose. But I had to be extremely delicate in my choice of language.

And I also had to be realistic. There would be fabulous girls at the gala, all wanting to meet him.

$$- 2 -$$

SO WHAT COULD I OFFER HIM that was different from most janes?

Perhaps a literary intensity?

A subtle film knowledge eliciting seductiveness?

Or could I simply radiate Gotham's birthright—the city's remarkable energy?

I felt heady, almost hallucinatory. I had to approach this man with extreme delicacy. He was the ultimate romantic hero for sophisticated ladies.

What did I have in my arsenal of sex tricks?

Seductiveness was not an aphrodisiac I'd had much training in (except for that remarkable one-time date with Harry.) Usually I simply shimmied a bit and giggled at everything a man said as he courted me—not *veree* aggressive.

What the hell is sexual energy anyhow? Everyone is always prattling on about sexual chemistry.

But what is it really?

− 3 −

FANCY HAD HER STYLE. She'd say, "Let's cruise SoHo, where we'll pick up some really charged guys."

FANCY'S CHECKLIST:

What kind of scarf did he wear?
Was his hair moussed properly?
What was the paperback book in his pocket?
Were his nails manicured?
How tight were his jeans?
And did his bazooka show?
If yes, how large did it seem?

But I had no such checklist. I simply looked at a guy's eyes. If they were blue and he was slim . . . if he had a decidedly acerbic wit and spoke semi-Brit English in a very royal-family way, that was it.

How sad was I?

I'm not a ninny. I knew in my heart this was an incurable crush.

Still, to be truthful, I couldn't help thinking about it.

Suppose . . .

— 4 —

TIME TO ACT.

I chose a satin deep bronze clinging top which would match Gran's fabulous amber necklace, cutting the v-neck a smidgen so the beads would nestle on my breasts.

I needed a bronze-colored bra. My lingerie wardrobe produced bras of pink, blue, black, brown, red, polka-dot, gray, leopard, fuschia and orange—but no bronze.

No problem. Victoria's Secret was down the street. I'd wear my outfit and stop in there for the most sexy decollete I could find.

Now for the rest. I chose a long satin skirt with a slit up to my crotch—a look both sexy and ladylike. I searched for the satiny bronze-colored pantyhose I'd hidden. After rummaging under three piles of undies, I found them. They would look great with the pink satin vintage Gucci mules I was saving for New Year's Eve.

Oh-oh. I didn't have bronze panties, either. Okay, Victoria's Secret could solve that problem also.

Now for a bath. Peppermint and musk droplets would be really sexy and aloe vera soap had an enticing scent. I luxuriated for only twenty minutes because I didn't want to be late.

Oh, but I was. Quickly, I phoned Harry and explained I had to do an errand. Could I meet him at the entrance of the SoHo hotel where the gala was to take place?

"Yes, of course," he said. "I'll be wearing a black tux."

Now the makeup. My own stash was limited, but Mom left a bag of freebies in case of emergencies.

First, I plucked my eyebrows. I went overboard and ended

up with them too thin. Damn! It was a little scary. I had to use a pencil to arch them.

I selected a makeup stick which promised to screen out all imperfections, added a makeup base, heightened my cheeks with sequined rouge sheen, and smeared sharp pink gloss onto my lips. For my eyes I tried black mascara and blue eye shadow. Then I moussed my hair and shook it out with a ferocious jolt to get it more voluminous.

I checked my face.

Wow!!

I looked like one of those *Vogue* magazine models.

I put on the blouse, sans bra. I wasn't very heavy in the bosom department, but without a bra, this top made me look like I was breast-feeding.

Not to worry. Victoria's Secret would fix that. Quickly, I donned a pair of cotton panties for temporary duty, then the skirt, pantyhose and mules.

Voila.

Did I look too chunky? Unsure, I turned and twirled in front of the mirror. Should I wear something more punk, perhaps a downtown demimonde look? How about that Asian dress—the one sent by that Japanese director whose work I hated? He said the vibes would do me in.

I preened in front of the mirror, posing with one leg cocked so the slit would open.

Really sassy.

When my Darling Lad looked at me, I wanted him to think, *I want to rip everything right off that girl!*

Interference.

(Comprised of JANO voices)

A CHORUS OF CONSCIENCE

Lizzie, what are you doing?
You're acting like a floozy
You're being weird
Remember, you're an Austen Girl
You are Harry's date
Your Lad is totally a fantasy
Wake up and smell the roses

My Jane Austen pals were right. But I simply didn't care. Tonight, I would meet my Prince Charming.

— 5 —

I STASHED TISSUES, LIP GLOSS, cash, and keys into a tiny sequined bag and left a messy apartment behind me. As I ran down the street to Victoria's Secret, my bosom bounced in a way that attracted the gaze of every man on the street.

Hell! The store was closed. They'd had a flood and were making repairs. A list of nearby stores was hung on the door. I checked my watch. I'd try for the one in SoHo.

I flagged a taxi. As I rushed into it, I heard a loud tear. Oh, no—my pantyhose! I checked my legs. Yes, I now wore bronze-colored tatters up and down my right leg. *Keep calm*, I told myself. I'd pick up a new pair at the shop.

"Prince Street and Broadway," I shouted to the driver.

"I'm not deaf, lady."

"Sorry. I'm late."

"Yeah, everybody's always late."

He drove down Seventh Avenue, then turned east onto Houston Street as far as Greene Street, where traffic was stalled because of a police investigation.

"I'd better get out here," I said.

I ran down Houston Street, coming round to Broadway, where I discovered it wasn't the police but Paragon Films that was restricting traffic in this part of town.

There were the usual scraggly types all over the place with walkie-talkies. An assistant director with a bullhorn stopped me. "You can't go there."

I didn't obey. I ran down the block, careful not to trip over the snarls of large wire as several Paragon monsters pursued me.

Then a loud voice called out, *"She's ruining the shot!"*

I reached the corner, where I discovered Victoria's Secret was in the shot and thus closed to the public.

Suddenly, large hands materialized around my torso, and I was shoved to one side of the street.

"Hey, watch that!" I warned.

"You just cost Paragon Studios thousands of dollars," Mr. Bullhorn accused.

Oh, hell.

I checked my watch. It was eight o'clock, and I still had to get to the hotel. If I walked briskly, I would only be five minutes late. I rushed, knowing that these galas started promptly when they were being televised.

Running . . . running . . . down the streets.

Finally, I spotted darling Harry pacing in front of the hotel. When he saw me, he gestured for me to be quick.

"Sorry," I said when I reached him.

Giving me a close-range inspection, he said, "What the hell is wrong with you, Lizzie? You look like a fright."

And he sounded quite scared.

− 6 −

IN THE LOBBY, HARRY TISSUED off some of my makeup. "Now you have the muted Da Vinci look," he said. "My Mona Lisa." He kissed me on the lips in front of all those prying eyes and clucking tongues. Then he took off his Brit scarf and wound it about my neck so that it draped in front of my bulging breasts.

"Native style not good for sophisticated gala," he mimicked Peter Sellers.

I melted into his arms when he added, "But Lizzie, you're adorable."

The air sizzled with excitement as we paraded into the banquet hall. The audience resembled those Merchant-Ivory films where people dressed to the nines took leisurely strolls up marble staircases, exuding charm as butlers announced their important names and titles.

"Why are we all so formal and important?" I asked Harry.

"We are the media royalty," he joked. "And we behave like that at this kind of occasion. We're the chosen people with a mandate to record and give opinions on entertainment news."

"Oh, sure," I retorted. "We live on a special plane above the earth. We're not really human, but a breed of star-meteor-android."

I gussied up. "And we must look very glamorous."

"Uh-huh." Harry laughed.

"And look at the dais. The gorgeous palm trees in the background, the overwhelming vases of water lilies, the velvet chairs, the elegant table setting. It looks like the Last Supper for film stars."

"It is what it is, Lizzie," Harry smirked. "And here's our table."

Around the table were colleagues—some were pals, some not. Luckily, Harry sat on my left and kept his arm around my shoulders in a protective stance.

Next to Harry was Lucretia Valdez, a famous set designer. As is customary with people who love ancient history, Ms. Valdez was swathed with a strange silkish robe no Roman lady would have been seen dead in.

Though her outfit was topped with a smashing garnet necklace and matching earrings fit for a queen, I did not feel jealous at all. Instead, I fingered my authentic amber beads, which caught her attention. Like a royal tiger reclining at the feet of Caesar, she growled at their luster.

Plump bald men in elegant tuxedos sat at the dais. The director of the festival, Stewart Epson, had the center seat. Alongside him was Valerie Anderson, who won an Oscar two years ago. They were chatting amiably, Valerie using her hands to make her point, as usual.

I watched carefully as more gorgeous ladies were seated at the dais. Finally the Last Supper was complete with its holy saints—the PRODUCERS and the STARS—occupying all but one seat at the end.

Could that be the Lad's spot? Why wasn't he in the center of the action?

I asked Martin Winders, who was sitting next to me. Martin was a columnist for *Living Film Magazine*.

"Oh, you know how he is . . ."

"No. How is he?" I interrupted.

"You've never met him?" I shook my head. "But you're so kind to him in your reviews."

"Ron assigns another reporter to do interviews. The boss maintains that a critic has to remain distant from the stars so as not to be influenced. In fact, I don't know any stars personally."

"Oh. Okay." Martin looked skeptical—he spent all his free time running with film stars.

That's when Martin surprised me. "I hear you're looking for a gig. They're in the market for someone over at *The New Gotham Magazine*."

I was puzzled. Martin was one of the main advocates of the auteur film claque—the group that regarded directors as gods. I'd often attacked that idea in print.

"You're not mad at me?"

"Nobody's mad at you, Lizzie, not even Ron. He's simply trying to get some salary leverage for when he offers you a new gig. It's normal media negotiations. Everybody does it. They tear you down so they can get you cheaper."

He shrugged his bony shoulders. "I'll call over and put a word in for you."

I was touched. "You will?"

"Sure."

I leaned over and kissed Martin, despite the fact that his face had pockmarks all over it. Sometimes a girl has to be bigger than kissing only handsome chaps.

Screeches from the lobby. I stood up immediately. Harry looked concerned. "Lizzie, it's better if you wait here."

I whispered. "I have to pee."

I wasn't lying. It was the truth. When I thought of my Darling Lad in the same room, my legs just wobbled.

I draped Harry's scarf so that my breasts wouldn't bounce as I walked out into the lobby. There, a chorus of girls wearing too-large sunglasses adorned with rhinestones, their midriffs uniformly peeking out of identical low-rise jeans, were screaming. A quartet of burly types was trying to keep order as the girls surrounded a rock star and several paparazzi snapped the chaos. Additional public relations types were running around the edges of the swarm, arms up, trying to get into the source of the ruckus. I caught a peek of one girl shrieking hysterically as one bodyguard tried to unclasp her hands from the star's ankle.

"The ladies room," I asked an usher.

He said, "Take a left, and you'll find an unmarked door which leads to a private one. Everything out here is overrun with fans." He sent a harried gaze toward the screaming cluster.

I nodded.

Following his instruction, I was about to push the leather door when it suddenly swung open and crashed into me.

Ohmigod!

As I rebounded off the wall, my Darling Lad came straight at me. His gorgeous blue eyes—the ones I yearned to gaze into—were wide with startled dismay as his body came into contact with mine.

His lips tightened. Oh, I'd love to pry them open with my hot tongue!

I felt the weight of his body against mine in a way I'd NEVER imagined.

POW!!!

WOW!!!

Just a split second before I hit the cold marble floor
I thought . . .
I'VE BEEN RAMMED BY MY DARLING LAD!

OH MY GOD!!!
This is
R E A L L Y   C O O L !!!

Chapter Twenty-six

— 1 —

He was riding fast into the wind that stirred his steed's mane. Yes, my knight on a white horse was coming to rescue me as I lay in a muddy patch on the side of the steep hill, just like Marianne in Sense and Sensibility.

Through the grey mist I could barely see him, but I knew he was the man who had stolen my heart. As he came closer, he leaped from his horse to kneel at my feet.

I called out, "Darling!" and looked into his beautiful blue eyes.

"Harry . . . ?"

"I'm here, Lizzie. How do you feel?"

"Terrible."

There was a buzz in my head as I tried to remember what happened.

"I'll make the pain go away," Harry said, kissing my forehead.

Dazed, I looked into his face. That's what my Dad used to say when I fell and hurt myself.

"Uh-huh."

"Well, you really fell for your Brit, didn't you?"

I seemed to be lying on the cold floor, but my head was cradled in Harry's lap. My eyes flicked around, searching.

"I guess."

"He sends his apologies. He had a plane to catch."

Damn!

"But he said you have a blank check. Anything you want—anything you need."

Well, that's a bit better.

(Hmmmmm. I wondered whether the Lad would honor my request to bed him if I couched it in the form of a need.)

"Is it very bad?" Harry asked, bending to kiss my fore-head again.

I looked at his face, so caring, so sweet.

"Nuh-uh," I lied bravely.

"Are you sure it doesn't hurt?" he asked tenderly.

"Y-yeah . . ."

"You know you have to give up running after this guy, don't you? After what happened, the fates are sending a message that the two of you are highly combustible."

"We are?"

Through the buzz in my head, I heard Edgar Meredith's throaty rasp. "You're seriously flawed, Lizzie. You've been try-ing to keep your head above water, but to tell the truth, you haven't managed too well. First it's the Brit. Then it's Harry. Then it's back to the Lad. Goddamn it, make up your mind."

"Oh, shut up!" I grumbled.

"What?" Harry said.

"Oh, I'm not talking to you, Harry."

"Lizzie, there's no one else here."

"Oh, yes, there is. There's you, and Mom, and the Lad, Edgar, and Gran . . . and now, there's Dad."

"Huh?"

That's when I began blabbing on about my family history,

about how infidelity ruined my parents' life and destroyed my childhood.

Oddly, Harry looked as if he really understood. "I know what you mean. My mother married three times, and I can't forget a single one of the bastards."

"They cheated on her?"

"No, the other way around. All three wrote plays that she starred in. When things went wrong offstage, the poor dopes would cry on my shoulder. I was just a kid, and I had to prop up these guys to forgive and forget." He paused. "That's how I learned about all this stuff."

He looked at me for a long moment, then said, "The thing is, Lizzie, that we go around searching out fantasies— not people. That's why things don't work out. But if you find someone who delights you, who makes you laugh, and if the kind of things you love delight her, too, you have a chance."

Then he added, "Anyway, it's a beginning. But there are always two or three dreams that each person still has, and why shouldn't it be that way? That's life."

"But what about love?"

"What about love?" he repeated.

"When you love someone, you're automatically jealous, aren't you?"

"Yes. But I can't be jealous of your crush on the Brit because it's only a fantasy. I knew all along that he was important to you because you were lonely and panicked and just plain bewildered about men. I knew you were programmed to be disappointed by love because you always adored every *Brief Encounter* type film you saw."

"Was I that obvious?"

"To me you were, because I was interested in you. And then we kind of stumbled into bed, and it was more than that. Somewhere between those silly lace sheets I fell for you."

Suddenly, my vision cleared. When I looked at Harry, it was as if a veil had lifted—a curtain that had stood between us, hiding us from each other.

I reached out to touch his face.

"Whaddaya say? Move in with me?" he said.

– 2 –

I DIDN'T KNOW WHAT TO DO. I do love Harry. I know that now.

But do I want to give up my independence?

Do I want to be the girl?

Then I remembered Gran's edict that everything in life can be negotiated.

"Well . . ."

"Oh, come on, Lizzie. Say yes."

"You're taking advantage of me. I can't think straight right now."

"That's right—I am."

"But can you forget all the stuff I put you through—about the exes, and—"

Harry's eyes looked teary, and his voice grew very soft. "Look, if you move in with me, you'll be my lady . . . I won't see anybody else."

"You won't?"

"Will you?"

"What? Come live with you or not see anybody else?"

"Both." He laughed. "Lizzie, you can bring over your Lad's posters."

"You won't mind?"

"Nope. You can have both of us, darling. But remember,

the Brit will always have a plane to catch and another girl to kiss."

"Yes."

"Good." Then he looked mischievous and said, "And I'll keep my Shania tapes. Fair?"

"Huh?"

"I just LOVE it when you wear *her* clothes."

— 3 —

OHMIGOD. Harry is *REALLY* Machiavellian.

He knows I'll never give up dreaming about my Darling Lad.

And he doesn't give a damn.

What a guy!

— 4 —

AND THAT'S ABOUT AS GOOD AS IT GETS FOR A JANE AUSTEN GIRL.

Chapter Twenty-seven

— 1 —

M ORAL:

ALWAYS AGREE WITH YOUR CUTIE WHEN HE ADORES YOU BUT HAVE A PHOTO OF YOUR SECRET LAD NEARBY

ALWAYS DREAM YOUR DREAMS WHILST READING JANE AUSTEN IN THE BATH

ALWAYS LIE LIKE A BITCH IN ANY SITUATION THAT INVOLVES YOUR FANTASIES

ALWAYS *REMEMBER* YOUR DREAMS ARE YOUR *VEREE* PRIVATE PLACE
AND THAT NO ONE—*ABSOLUTELY NO ONE*—
NEEDS TO KNOW
WHATEVER—OR WHOEVER—
YOU'RE *TRIPPING WITH* . . .

— 2 —

BUT
LET HIM HAVE HIS DREAMS, TOO

BE FAIR

— *The End* —